CM0892845

MARGARETTOWN

Margarettown

GABRIELLE ZEVIN

HODDER &
STOUGHTON

First published in 2005 by Miramax Books
First published in Great Britain in 2005 by Hodder & Stoughton
A division of Hodder Headline

The right of Gabrielle Zevin to be identified as the Author of the Work has been asserted
by her in accordance with the Copyright, Designs and Patent Act 1988.

1

A CIP catalogue record for this title is available from the British Library

Hardback ISBN 0 340 89645 0
Trade Paperback ISBN 0 340 89646 9

Printed and bound by Mackays of Chatham Ltd, Chatham, Kent

Hodder Headline's policy is to use papers that are natural, renewable and recyclable
products and made from wood grown in sustainable forests. The logging and manufac-
turing processes are expected to conform to the environmental regulations of the country of origin.

Hodder & Stoughton Ltd
A division of Hodder Headline
338 Euston Road
London NW1 3BH

CONTENTS

To M. & D.

I. *Maggie in Bed*

I.

When I first met Margaret, I lived in a basement apartment. The rent was reasonable, and the location was better than I might have afforded otherwise. The view from belowground was interesting, if not ideal: shoes and sometimes a bit of calf, small dogs, up to one-third of toddlers. I learned to recognize my own visitors by their shoes. At that time, my only regular callers were my sister, Bess, with her atrocious faux-suede sandals, and Margaret, whose footwear varied with her mood.

I lived a strange basement sort of life. Distinctions between night and day seemed less important. Insects and other vermin, unseen in respectable aboveground places, were my habitués. When snow melted, the apartment flooded. On garbage day, I had to keep my windows shut. The apartment refused to heat and maintained a year-round temperature of forty-six degrees. Even the tenants who lived above me seemed to approach me with suspicion. Living in a basement had somehow made me *that guy who lives in the basement*.

The only furniture I had I'd stolen from the university where I was a graduate student at the time. Instead of a real bed, I had two extra-long twin mattresses. When I slept alone, I stacked the mattresses on top of each other. When I had a guest, I laid them side by side and pushed them together. For the last year, my guest had been one Margaret Mary Towne. In those days, she was called Maggie.

Despite my best efforts, the mattresses would never stay together. A mysterious gap would always form between the two during the night. Maggie and I would end up adrift on those twins like castaways from a fifties television show. One night, she crawled into my twin. She claimed she was cold and she never left.

On the night after Maggie graduated from college (she was older than most of the students, twenty-five), I awoke to find her sitting in the gap between the mattresses. She was holding her knees to her chest and sobbing quietly. Her face was covered by her long, straight, red hair. I asked her what was wrong, and for the longest time, she didn't answer me.

"I'm cursed," she said finally.

"No, you're not," I said, and then thought better of it. "Well, what do you mean 'cursed'?"

"There're things about me," she insisted.

"What things, Maggie?"

"There're things about me. When you find them out, you're going to despise me, I know it."

I assured her that I couldn't despise her and that, in point of fact, I loved her.

"I'm not who you think I am. I mean, I am, but there're other parts, too. I'm only partly who you think I am. I'm not like other women."

"Oh Maggie," I said, "Maggie." I was thirty-one at the time, and her dilemma seemed adorably early twenties. "Maggie, everyone goes through this when they graduate."

She peered out from under her veil of hair. She shook her head and shot me a withering look indeed. "If things change after tomorrow... If things change for the worse, I mean... This time we had, these months were perfectly gorgeous. I loved this basement. I loved *us* in this basement."

She kissed me on the forehead in what I felt was a slightly condescending manner and, for the first time since her migration, returned to the other bed to sleep.

For the rest of the night she slept soundly but I, having been woken, did not. I lay awake, thinking of her. For all I knew, this had been her intent.

I thought of Maggie on Commonwealth last December. We'd slept together once at the time, and I wasn't sure if we were going to again. She laughed when she saw me and called my name. She didn't wait for me to see her first.

"I'm glad I wore my good boots after all," she said. "I was on my way out the door. I was wearing my winter clogs, but I decided to change at the last moment."

I looked at her shoes. They were thin, black leather, pointy in the toe and heel, not very insulated. "These are your good boots?" I asked.

She laughed. "Compared to my clogs, yes. Maybe you don't agree?" And she laughed again. "I had that feeling you get when you know you're about to run into your ex or some other man you should like to be handsome around. I didn't know it would be you."

"If you had, would you still have worn them?"

She cocked her head and smiled slowly. "I would have," she said, "yes."

That slow smile. Jesus Christ.

In the other twin, Maggie snored, and I thought of her on the day I told her I loved her.

"I love you," I said. A car honked just as I said it, censoring me. I wasn't sure if she had heard me and I had to repeat myself. "I love you."

She seemed to be perplexed or pleased (on Maggie's face, always slightly opaque, these emotions could register the same way), but she said nothing. After a moment, she ran down the street.

Six or so hours later, the phone rang. "I love you," she said, and then she hung up.

As for the gap, did it make it mean more or less? Had there been no gap, I would have known she was saying it by instinct, which could be good or bad. After all, if you shoot at a man, he will try to shoot you, too. With the gap, I knew it was not instinct. I knew she had considered my own declaration of love and her response to it for the better part of six hours. A lengthy deliberation, yes, but in the end, there was good reason to believe she had meant what she said.

When I told her I loved her, I was expressing an emotion that I did not quite feel at the time. I think

I wanted to hear her response more than anything. Or maybe, I just wanted to say it. Sometimes, we lie optimistically. Sometimes, we say what is not quite true with the hope that it will become true. This time, it worked; I loved her for that gap.

From the window in my bedroom, I could see that the sidewalk looked light gray, which meant it was getting late or early, depending on one's point of view. I wouldn't be sleeping tonight. So instead, I thought of Maggie in bed, and how the first time I met her she was lying down.

Before I met her, I had seen her name (TOWNE, MARGARET M.) on a list of other meaningless names. She was a student in the section of a required philosophy course I was TA-ing. The semester was half over, and she hadn't shown up to discussion section once or even bothered to buy the course packet. I left messages for her, sent letters, made a show of doing the things a teaching assistant is supposed to do. At that time, the university was championing a policy of "personal attention": that U was really a small liberal arts college in the body of a large institution or some such nonsense. The policy meant I was supposed to at least meet TOWNE, MARGARET M. before I failed her.

She lived in a certain cinderblock dorm that was known for housing U's misfits: the marrieds, the exchange students, the transfers, the "mature" students, etc. Every college has such a dorm. I took the elevator to her room with this reputation in mind.

On her floor, several indeterminately foreign students were having a party. I was offered a bowl of a red and bubbly food by a girl in a leotard. I politely declined but asked if she could point me in the direction of Margaret Towne. With a sigh, the girl gestured down the hall.

Her name was written in purple ink on a dry erase board on her door. The top half of the "M" in Margaret and all of the "e" in Towne were erased. The handwriting was old-fashioned and precise, as if the writer had been taught penmanship (and probably not much else) in a one-room schoolhouse. I prepared myself for an empty-headed rich girl of the type that abounded at U.

I knocked on the door and, to my surprise, it swung open. The room was nine by seven, cinderblocks on three sides, rather like a prison cell.

There wasn't much space for anything other than the standard-issue extra-long twin bed. Seven or so mattresses were stacked on the bed frame. Atop the pile was Margaret Towne herself. Her long red hair was tangled and slightly matted. She had dark circles under her eyes and looked on the verge of tears or laughter, or maybe just exhaustion. [Jane, you might get the idea that seven mattresses would raise a person quite high, but U's mattresses were exceedingly paltry. Seven of U's were roughly the equivalent of two anywhere else in the world.]

"I'm so tired," she said. "I feel like I haven't slept in years and years."

"Margaret, I'm the teaching—"

She interrupted me. "You look tired yourself."

The way she said it, I almost felt like crying. "I am," I said. "I am tired."

"You can sleep here if you want," she offered.

"Here in your bed?" I was incredulous.

"Here in my bed."

And so I did. Offers like hers don't come around every day.

I woke up the next afternoon, a Friday. She was looking at me.

"How did you sleep?" she asked.

"Well." I yawned. "Margaret, what's with all the mattresses?"

"I thought they would help me sleep, but it hasn't really worked," she said as she got out of bed. "I'm going to brush my teeth. I wanted to go before, but I hated to wake you."

I lay in Margaret's bed, feeling the happiness of the well-rested. I shifted to the center, and that's when I felt it—a lump. A small, but palpable, lump. I got out of bed and lifted up the first mattress. Nothing. Then the second. Nothing. And then the third, fourth, fifth, sixth. Nothing, nothing, nothing, nothing. And finally, I lifted the seventh mattress, the one next to the bed frame. And that's when I found it—a pen. An ancient black Bic, slightly chewed on one end, the kind that comes ten for a dollar.

She reentered the room and cocked her head.

I held the offending object out to her. "You were sleeping on a pen."

"A pen," she said with a laugh. "Oh." She took the pen from me and looked at it for a long, long time. She kissed me and thanked me and kissed me again. She happily returned to bed and invited me to join her. I did, Jane, I did.

"Margaret," I began.

"I'm called Maggie," she said. "When you say Margaret, I barely know who you're talking to." She smiled her slow, sleepy smile and rolled onto her side. "The pen. I wonder if it still writes."

"Probably not. It looks pretty old."

She persisted. "I wonder if it does, though."

I saw where this was going, so I got out of bed and found a sheet of loose-leaf paper. To rouse the ink, I began doodling a sloppy infinity sign.

"Looks dead," I said after about a minute. The paper was starting to rip from the pressure and the repetition.

"Keep trying," she said. "Please," she said.

And so I kept trying. I switched to a heart. And then the alphabet. And then I wrote my name. It was then that the pen started to work.

Margaret laughed. "I'm so happy," she said. "I don't know why I'm so happy, but I am." She looked at the pen like it was the first pen ever. She looked at me like I was the inventor of the first pen ever. "Is that your name?" she asked, inspecting my work.

"It is," I said.

"It's a good name. I'm glad it's your name. It's a good, solid name."

"Thank you, I guess."

"The pen, it seems like a good sign, doesn't it?"
I agreed that it did.

She read my name again and then she nodded.
"You're the teaching assistant for Moral Reasoning,
aren't you?"

"I am," I admitted reluctantly. "The head teaching assistant actually."

"It's total bullshit, isn't it?"

"It is," I agreed.

"It is," she repeated. "Now, why don't you come
back to bed?"

And then I slept, but my heart was awake. She
had this way of making you think that you were the
first man who had ever discovered this particular
plot of land.

The sidewalk was turning a yellowish color, which
meant I had been up all night. I looked over at Maggie. Her red hair was everywhere; her eyes were
puffy; her breath was awful; she had a hint of mustache. All at once, I wanted to spend the rest of my
life with this woman, cursed or not. There was
nothing that could happen, nothing she could say

or not say, nothing she had done or would do, that would change it. It was 5 A.M., and I was sure.

Maggie had moved out of the dorm the week before. Her boxes lined the walls of my bedroom. (She had fit a surprising amount in that nine-by-seven cell.) On top of the box labeled MARGARET TOWNE—MISC. were a large ball of twine and a knife, among other packing supplies. I got out of bed and cut a three-inch piece of twine. Then I crawled into her bed and considered my girl as she lay naked atop the sheets.

One leg was bent and the other was straight, but both roads led to the same place: a small grassy hill in yellows and browns like wheat, secreting a well. (In those days, I liked to imagine that only I knew the location of that well.) And then, the plain of her stomach—smooth and vast and soft and not quite flat. Across the plain were two more small hills— lovely, lovely. And between those lovely hills, her neck was a narrow, white path. And her eyes were closed, but I knew they looked brown in some lights and gold in others. And she smelled like apples, and her cheeks burned like a set of porch lights, and her hair was red like faded tiles on a Spanish roof. And all this land would be mine, I thought as I tied a bow around her finger.

"What are you doing?" she asked drowsily.

"It's so I don't forget."

"Forget what?" she asked.

"The thing I want to remember."

"Shouldn't you tie it around your own finger, then?"

"Go back to sleep. We've got a long day tomorrow."

She flipped onto her stomach. A second later, she rolled onto her side and smiled at me. "I've made room for you," she said. "If you want it, there's room."

2.

While Maggie was still asleep, I sneaked out to retrieve Uncle Jacques's blue convertible. Although Uncle Jacques had been dead for many years at the time and the car had been bequeathed to me, I still thought of it as his convertible. Uncle Jacques had driven convertibles his whole life, and always with the top down. When asked about this predilection, he liked to say in his cartoonish Belgian accent, "The rain, it may fall, but certainly not on me, no?" And then he would laugh like an idiot, like he hadn't given the same response a thousand times before. When I was sixteen, a history book reported that one of the French kings (Louis XIII? XV?) had said, "*Après moi, le déluge,*" which sounded exactly like something Uncle Jacques would say. Indeed, for all of European History, I saw Uncle Jacques's face in the place of any French despot. It was a particularly satisfying fantasy when Louis (XVI? XVII?) was beheaded toward the end of the spring term.

After our parents' deaths, my sister, Bess, and I had nowhere to go, and Uncle Jacques, my mother's brother, took us in. I knew I should be grateful and sometimes I even was.

Picking up the car meant having breakfast with Bess. (The car was parked in her apartment complex's garage.) In those days, Bess was very concerned about *things*. She wrote letters to editors of magazines; she marched in rallies; she made fliers and signs (and always recycled aforementioned fliers and signs); she attended meetings; she chained herself to buildings; she checked labels; she worried excessively about her brother; in short, she did every single thing a person *should* do.

Over breakfast, I informed Bess that I was taking the car to help Maggie move her college possessions back home.

Bess furrowed her brow and said, "I'm very concerned about *things*." What *things*, she chose not to specify, and I knew enough not to ask. She would tell me eventually anyway. "I'm very concerned about *things*," she repeated, scooping porridge into bowls. [Jane, I'm not sure how porridge truly differs from oatmeal; I believe porridge has more integrity than oatmeal, which is why I associate porridge with your aunt.]

We ate for five minutes without speaking. When Bess couldn't stand it any longer, she said, "I'm very concerned about the way you're choosing to live your life."

Once again, no response was required from me.

"I love you," she said, "but I'm very concerned."

"I'm thinking of asking Maggie to marry me," I told her.

Bess sighed and began clearing the table.

"Actually, I think I already have."

"Have you or haven't you?" Bess demanded.

"I'm not sure."

"You ought to know one way or the other," she said.

I hesitated. "Well, if she remembers, then I did. And if she thinks I did, then I did. But I never really did. Not in so many words. I suppose I wouldn't mind if she thought I had."

Bess shook her head and then hugged me. As she opened her mouth to speak, I realized I couldn't possibly stand to hear what she had to say. "Maggie and I have to get on the road if we're to make it to her house at a reasonable hour," I said.

"Where does she live?" Bess asked.

"I'm not sure." Indeed, she had only said that it was far, but in driving distance.

Bess sighed and opened her mouth to speak.

"You're going to say I ought to know where she's from before I marry her."

"For your information, I was going to say that if you have a choice in routes, you should avoid 95 for the next couple of hours because there's been an accident with an oil truck. Although it would certainly be good to find out where she lives before you attempt to drive there."

"Maggie'll be in the car with me. She can direct me."

"And if she falls asleep?"

"I'll wake her."

Bess shook her head. "I'm concerned," she said, "very concerned."

As long as she was concerned already, I decided to ask the one thing I really wanted to know. "When a woman says she's 'cursed,' what does she mean?"

"Um, like menstruation?"

"I don't think so."

"*Cursed*? Who's *cursed*?"

"No one. I only meant, does the word 'cursed' have a special connotation? For women, I mean?"

"Did Maggie say she was 'cursed'?"

"Of course not. It's for my work," I insisted pathetically. "I'm translating one of Arendt's letters."

Bess raised an eyebrow. "When a woman says she's 'cursed,' the only thing to do is take her at her word."

The one time Bess had met Maggie was accidentally, at a movie theater. Maggie and I were going to see one movie; Bess was on her way out from another.

"You must be L_____," Bess said. (L_____ was my girlfriend before Maggie.)

"She isn't," I said quickly. "She's Maggie."

"Are you going to see that one?" Bess indicated the theater to her right.

"Yes," I said.

"It's awful," Bess said, "but *he* likes to see crap." She looked Maggie up and down. "Your hair is very red," she said.

"I know," Maggie conceded.

"You look more like a L_____ than a Maggie," Bess said to her. "Is your real name Margaret?"

Maggie paused before she said, "Sometimes."

❧

We packed Maggie's things into the backseat of Jacques's convertible. The box labeled MARGARET TOWNE—MISC. wouldn't fit, so she left that at my apartment. We were on the road by 3 P.M.

Before we got into the car, she held up her hand. The string was still tied around her ring finger. I was beginning to doubt the wisdom of that string.

"I'm engaged," she said.

"With what?" I asked coyly.

She held up her left hand. "So I don't forget," she said.

"So you don't forget what exactly?"

"That I'm engaged."

I looked at the string; it was already beginning to fray. "It's fraying."

She shrugged. "I know. I've been meaning to tape the ends." She removed a roll of packing tape from her pocket and cut two narrow strips. "Would you help me? It's difficult with only one hand."

"Why don't you just untie it?"

"Oh no, I could never do that." She shook her head and handed me one of the pieces. "You see, when he asked me, he tied that bow himself."

"You could untie it and retie it, and he would never know the difference."

"I would know the difference," she said, "and I would need someone else to do the retying."

"Your boyfriend—"

"My fiancé," she corrected me, "fiancé." She liked saying that word, "fiancé."

"Your fiancé must be a bastard."

"My fiancé's wonderful."

"Or he's cheap." I finished taping the second end. "I'm done."

"Thank you," she said. "And my fiancé's not at all cheap."

"One ball of twine and this guy could marry half the gals in Boston."

"My fiancé would never do that." She was injured; I could tell.

"I'm sorry."

"Do you honestly think the ring makes a difference anyway? Plenty of men have bought plenty of women plenty of rings and . . ." Her voice trailed off.

"No, you're right," I said. "Before, I was only joking with you."

"I like my piece of string," she insisted. I took her hand, and she took it back. "Now you've made me feel cheap," she said with a rueful smile.

"That wasn't my intent," I said.

"Maybe it *is* stupid." She sighed. "Why don't men wear engagement rings? It's offensive when you think about it."

I shook my head.

"An engagement ring is really just a scarlet letter."

"Or a chastity belt," I added.

She laughed. "We auctioned off a couple of those last year. I found them myself in an old barn in Pennsylvania." Maggie had recently finished an internship at an auction house; back then, she had wanted to be an appraiser.

"Who bought them?"

"A professor from the Women's Studies Department at U bought one, and a dealer who specialized in those sorts of items took the second, and, I don't know why, but I bought the third."

I raised an eyebrow.

"No one else wanted it. I felt bad for it, I guess. It's in the box marked MISC., if you ever want to borrow it."

"I'll keep that in mind."

"Have you ever noticed that the word 'engaged' is in the past tense?" she asked. "Well, not technically. I mean, 'engaged' can be the past tense or past participle of the verb 'engage,' but when referring to marriage, 'engaged' is an adjective. The 'd' at the end makes it seem awful somehow, don't you think?"

"It would be so easy for me to untie that," I said, looking at her makeshift ring. "He ought to have bought you a real one, so it wouldn't be so easy to untie."

She nodded and stuck her other pinky in the loop of the bow. "When you think about it, a real ring could just slip off anyway. I'd have to make a real decision to remove this one."

"Or someone would." I leaned down and kissed her hand and took one of the taped ends between my teeth. It was harder to untie than I thought, but she didn't stop me. "Ought to have double-knotted it," I said.

"Next time, my fiancé will," she answered.

"How do you know he wasn't kidding?" I asked.

She narrowed her eyes. "What do you mean?"

"I mean, if all he gave you was a piece of string, how do you know he was serious?"

She laughed. "I suppose I don't," she said. "I thought he was, but I can't be sure." She laughed again. "And the truth is, I'm not sure that it matters much anyway."

[In retrospect, Jane, that string may have been

somewhat premature. But in my defense, I knew enough about her to know I wanted to know everything else; I knew as much about her as she wanted me to know; I knew as much about her as anyone ever knows about anyone. And isn't love just curiosity at the beginning anyway? What makes a person keep reading a book? First sentence? Not bad. Chapter one? All right. By the time you're almost at three, why *not* keep reading?]

She got into the passenger seat and slammed the door. "You drive the first leg," she said.

"Where do you live anyway?" I asked.

"It's in upstate New York between Marlboro and Newburgh," she said. "It's easy to get lost around there, so I'll have to do the last bit." And then she put her head against the window and closed her eyes.

"This might seem strange," she said, her eyes still shut, "but I actually have the same name as the place I'm from. I figured I'd tell you now, so it isn't a surprise."

"What do you mean?"

"I'm from a place called Margarettown," she said. "It's not a big deal; I just thought it might seem strange if I didn't mention it."

I looked at her to see if she was in earnest: her eyes

were closed, but the set of her mouth seemed earnest enough. I don't know why, but I laughed. "I assume you were named for the town and not vice versa."

She laughed, too. "I've never been completely sure."

We checked into a motel somewhere in Connecticut. Maggie wanted to stay at this particular motel because the sign promised A WATERBED IN EVERY ROOM, and neither of us had ever slept in one.

The room managed to be both damp and smoky. Maggie's waterbed was heart-shaped and seemed slightly deflated in the middle. Near the foot of the bed was a sinister water mark. The overall effect was more cheap motel in Vegas than cheap motel in Connecticut. We were both exhausted and retired without much discussion.

We lay in the dark. The more we tried to stay still, the more the bed kept rocking. I was tired, but I couldn't fall asleep.

"Close your eyes," she said.

I did.

"It's easy to imagine we're on a boat," she whispered. "It's easy to imagine we're lost at sea."

"What did you mean when you said you were cursed?" I asked.

"What did you mean when you tied that string around my finger?" she replied.

"It was a gesture," I said weakly.

"Do you see?" she asked. "You can't listen too much to anything anyone says in bed."

"That sounds like a fortune cookie," I said. "You can't listen to anything anyone says . . . *in bed*."

Maggie groaned (amicably, I think), and I rode the crest of the resulting wave.

3.

Bess says I ought to write more plainly and not try to make it like a novel. I ask her, What has she ever written that makes her such an expert? And she says, You don't need to be a writer to know from good writing.

She says, The best writing is clear, precise, and not overly poetic.

I say, sarcastically, Like *TV Guide*?

She says, Yes like *TV Guide,* in that *TV Guide*'s style is perfectly suited to its subject.

Furthermore, she says there's too much about Margaret and me in bed, and that no child wants to read that much about her parents in bed.

I say, What does she know about child rearing?

She says, I raised you, didn't I?

The thing that bothers me the most, she says, is the part about your apartment at the beginning. I remember that apartment, she says. I remember it very well, and the windows there were very high.

So? I say.

Well, she says, you describe seeing the sun on the sidewalk while you're presumably still lying in bed. And I'm telling you, you couldn't see out those windows while lying down. The angle wouldn't be right.

Oh Bess, I say, it's dramatic license. I needed to find a way to express that time was passing.

Well, I think you ought to be accurate, she says.

Everyone uses dramatic license, and anyone who says he doesn't is a liar.

And, she says, I never chained myself to a building. And I never thought she was L_____; I am very aware of the difference between L_____ and Margaret. And the first time I met Margaret wasn't at the movies. It was dinner at my apartment. And Uncle Jacques wasn't dead then. I can't confirm or deny the other parts because I wasn't there. But it doesn't sound at all like Margaret to invite someone she didn't even know into her bed. And what's with the "cursed" business? I don't remember that at all. Not at all.

This is my version, I tell my sister. It's lucky that you'll be around to tell Jane your own version anytime you please.

And you shouldn't write that you stole furniture from U.

Bess, I say, this is only for Jane. Besides which,

it was fifteen years ago. I really doubt that anyone's going to be tracking me down. And if they do try to, I'll be gone in six months anyway.

Don't say that, she says. Please don't say that.

I'm dying, I say. It's a dirty trick, but there's no getting around it.

I did appreciate that part about the porridge, Bess says in a softer voice. I always thought of it as gruel myself.

And she finally leaves me alone. And I admit it, I'm glad to see her go. Which isn't to say she doesn't have a point about the prose. It's true; I ought to state my purpose more clearly.

Jane, I write to you because your mother is dead and I am dying.

After my death, you will live with your aunt Bess, who is a lovely and sensible woman. Of course, Bess is not really your aunt in the biological sense. (A quick survey of Bess's bountiful bosom and hips should confirm this point beyond doubt.) Nonetheless I encourage you to call her Aunt Bess. In this life, Jane, pretend family is often the best you can do.

Your mother died when you were six, which is not something to feel at all sad about. You came to her late in life, and she was perfectly delighted with your arrival.

Do not blame us too much for naming you Jane. Jane may seem like the sort of a name parents saddle a child with when they are too bored or inattentive to come up with a better one. In your case though, a great deal of thought went into the selection of Jane. Your mother loathed nicknames (her own name was the endlessly nicknameable Margaret) and wanted to provide you with a name mostly devoid of them. "A Jane is always a Jane is always a Jane," she said on the occasion of your birth. And from my point of view, there was (and is) nothing wrong with being a "plain Jane," if by "plain," one means honest, unpreten- tious, and steadfast. I have always wanted to be these things myself, without much success.

Your mother, Margaret, was born in the year 19_ in Margarettown. (Whether she was named for the town or the town named for her, I have never been completely sure.) Her middle name was Mary. "If only I had been called Mary Margaret instead of Margaret Mary," she once said, "I suspect my life would have been much easier." Margaret's last name was Towne until the day she took my own. Not long after, she returned it to me and was Margaret Towne once more and forever.

She was born Margaret. As a girl, she was May; as a teenager, Mia; as an adult, Marge. When she died, she was Margaret once again. There were other iterations along the way: Old Margaret with the gray hair, the sexy and impossible Maggie whom I adored, the manic depressive Greta, and others, so many others. There were so many Margaret Townes. Sometimes I ask myself, How could Margaret have been so many women at once? And the answer is, Jane, that your mother was either a most extraordinary woman or a most ordinary one.

I knew all these Margaret Townes, and now they are all gone. Should I admit that I loved most, but not all, of them? Perhaps if I had managed to love Marge, even a little, the other Margarets might have stayed longer. Perhaps—but I get ahead of myself.

Our story really begins with the arrival of a most disreputable character in Margarettown: me. Yes, Jane, it is true. Once upon a time, your own beloved father was a cheat, a liar, and an all-around bastard. I was what is known as a cad. Much as I hate to admit it, I was, at times, the villain in this story. At other times, I was the love interest. In life, the villain and the love interest are the same person more often than you might think. It has been said that the lover is usually a thief, and indeed, it is difficult to love someone without robbing them of something. If you were older, you might argue with me. You might say that real love steals nothing. You might say that real love leaves a person intact. You would be wrong, Jane. Love is a greedy toddler who knows only the word "mine."

Although, Jane, when you were a toddler you knew many other words besides "mine." One of your particular favorites (it may have even been your first) was "lemon."

4.

Back on the road, Maggie said, "When I said I was cursed, I only meant that my family was a bit eccentric. I think I was just nervous about you meeting them."

"That makes sense," I said.

"My"—she paused—"my aunts have this crazy notion that I went to college to catch a man."

"Oh, that sort of thing's still pretty typical, I imagine."

"Is it?" Her voice was hopeful.

"Among women of a certain generation. Yes, I think it is."

"My aunts are old-fashioned, but I think I was being overly dramatic." She laughed. "Sometimes things seem so unbearable in the middle of the night, don't they? In the middle of the night, we're all such children."

I nodded. "So, it's interesting that you and the town have the same name."

"Yes," she said.

"Is there a story?"

"Yes," she said.

"Would you like to tell it?"

"At some point, maybe," she said. "Tell me when you want me to drive, by the way."

"Okay," I said.

"Oh, and there won't be any men there," she said.

"Where?"

"At my house. They're all dead or gone. Gone, more than dead."

"Are you trying to tell me something?" I asked.

"No," she said, "I was just informing you. We know so little about each other really."

[It might seem strange to you that Margaret and I had never spoken in detail about our families. Having had something of an unhappy childhood myself, I tend not to push people to tell me about theirs. It is a lie that people who love each other must know everything about each other. Love must occasionally allow for a gap.]

At around noon, she took over the driving. It occurred to me that I had never before been her passenger. The road was intricate and twisty.

"We always joke," Maggie said, "that the only way to get to Margarettown is to try to get lost."

We drove past an apple orchard. The fruit appeared ripe even though it was the beginning of summer. "I didn't know you could get apples this time of year," I said.

"Now you know," she said. She pulled the car over to the side of the road. She picked an apple from a branch that was hanging over the orchard fence and held it out to me. I took a bite.

"It's good," I said, and she handed me the rest. In fact, it wasn't a very good apple at all. The first bite had been deceptively sweet, but as I approached the core, it grew more and more bitter.

She turned on the radio and a familiar song came on:

> And it ain't no use in turnin' on your light, babe
> That light I never knowed
> And it ain't no use in turnin' on your light, babe
> I'm on the dark side of the road

"I love this song," she said. "I've heard it a million times, but I wouldn't mind hearing it a million more, you know?" She turned up the volume.

> But I wish there was somethin' you would do or say
> To try and make me change my mind and stay

We never did too much talkin' anyway
But don't think twice, it's all right

"I could listen to this song the rest of my life," she said. "Every time I hear it, it's different somehow."

"Or maybe you're different?" I suggested.

"Maybe," she said.

"What's the story of Margarettown?" I asked.

"Oh, all stories are the same, aren't they? Men and women fall in love or out of love. People are born; people die. It all ends happily or it all ends sadly, and the difference matters only to the people involved." She honked the horn three times, like an ellipsis, and we were back on the road. "In a way," she said, "they're all the same men and women anyway."

Most places are the same, too. The only way you ever know you've arrived anywhere is by the presence of a sign. I am now going to describe the Margarettown sign although, in point of fact, I didn't see it until nearly a month after my arrival there.

The sign (unremarkable, faded, wooden) read WELCOME TO and then in larger letters below, _ARGARETTOW_ (the "M" and the "N" apparently having abandoned the town with everyone else). The sign was like signs of its kind everywhere. At the bottom, where the population should have been, was an indecipherable two-digit palimpsest. The population might have been OO or 99; I could not be sure except to say that it had never reached three digits. An ordinary traveler would not consider the sign, or indeed the town, for very long. Margaret-town was very much the kind of place one passes through on one's way elsewhere. Make two or three wrong turns anywhere and you shall end up somewhere like it.

I had had very little sleep for the last two nights, and I dozed off not long after our stop in the orchard. As I had never before been Maggie's passenger and knew relatively little about her driving acumen, perhaps it wasn't wise that I had removed my seat belt for greater comfort.

I slipped into what was for me a recurring dream at that time. Indeed, it recurred so often, I actually wrote it down in a Dream Journal that Bess had given me the previous Christmas. [Your aunt always buys the worst gifts; I almost look forward to them because they are so bad.] Here is what I wrote:

I am on a mattress in the middle of the ocean. I am having sex with a woman, but I'm not sure who she is. I can't see her face because her hair (which is light, either blond or red) conceals it. I keep trying to pull the hair back, but it's difficult. When I finally succeed, I find she has no face. Sometimes, there is a variation where her face becomes a mirror, and I can see myself, only I'm a very old man.

I found this dream to be incredibly annoying because of its frequency, its heavy-handed symbolism, and its melodramatic portentousness. Our dreams are always so juvenile and embarrassing.

When I awoke from the dream, I found that Maggie had fallen asleep at the wheel, literally, and we were on the verge of driving off a small, wooden bridge into a river below.

I tried to rouse her. "Wake up!" I yelled.

A second later, another voice answered me, "Wake up, wake up, wake up, wake up," but it wasn't Maggie's. Indeed, the voice was my own, although I didn't recognize it at first. I would learn later that Margarettown had an echo.

"Maggie!" I yelled. "Margaret!"

"Margaret Margaret Margaret Margaret Margaret," the echo repeated.

I shook her, and Maggie finally opened her eyes.

She smiled at me, sweet and sleepy. "I was having the most lovely dream," she said.

"Dream dream dream dream dream," the echo replied.

"Maggie, we're going to die!"

"Die die die die die," the echo taunted.

"Oh fuck," she said.

"Fuck fuck fuck fuck fuck," the echo laughed.

At the last possible moment, Maggie slammed on the brakes. Her maneuver saved Jacques's convertible and herself from any significant injury. Having removed my seat belt, I was not quite as lucky.

Don't be frightened, Jane. I don't die here. I die toward the end of my story like any good narrator should. Here, my only significant injury is a leg broken in three places.

Originally, I had planned to drop Maggie off at her house, meet her folks, stay for a couple days tops, and return to my basement to work on my dissertation. But obviously, this isn't what happened. I ended up spending the whole summer (it may have been longer) in Margarettown.

So, darling, curl up and I shall tell you a story. I am told this story resembles a fairy tale, but then most of these kinds of stories do (at least in their beginning parts). If it seems implausible from time to time, I apologize. Some parts I have forgotten; some parts I have chosen to forget. The man who has no memory makes one out of paper. (I believe this is a quote, but I have forgotten whose.)

But enough with the disclaimers. The only way to begin is the only way one ever begins such things.

II. *Once Upon a Time*

I.

I do not remember who told me that the house was called Margaron. Maybe no one told me? Maybe I just read it somewhere? I don't recall if the house had a sign out front or not. Those early days in Margaret-town are a blur.

I do not remember being brought to Margaron either. (It is strange to arrive somewhere and have no idea how you got there.) Assembling the memory of arrival from various other memories, I imagine that it would have been something like this:

You drive over a bridge that is over a lake and next to a cliff. Past the bridge, two parallel dirt roads veer apart, but ultimately lead to the same place—a well. Past the well are two small hills, and over and between the two hills is Margaron herself.

Under some lighting conditions, the house looks beige and under others, almost yellow. The house is three stories, but viewed from the east, it looks like one. An addition, an afterthought, spoils the west side. Unlike other houses in the area, Margaron has an incongruous red roof made from Spanish tiles. The front yard is smooth and vast and not quite flat. A narrow white path leads to the front door, which is painted the same red as the roof. Two lanterns hang on both sides of the door. Although you couldn't see it from the front, the backyard is completely torn apart. (At some point, there were plans to build a pool.)

Because I was not given a formal tour of Margaron at the beginning, I never quite got a handle on her geography. I was constantly discovering something new. Was there always a lake? Was there always a treehouse in the front yard? Was there always a bathroom on the third floor?

Margaron seemed malleable, but perhaps all women are this way.

2.

When I finally woke a week or so after the accident, I was installed on the first floor of Margaron in what I thought was the guest bedroom. I later found out it was Marge's room, and she was none too happy to be lending it to me.

My leg was suspended above me in a cast, and a very old woman was seated at my bedside.

The woman was so old, she was past what I considered to be a woman. I guessed she must have been close to one hundred. Her eyes were a watery brown. Her teeth were yellow (the real ones) and sparkling white (the fake ones). Her nails were long and filed into sharp points. She was chopstick thin and wore a dark tweed suit with support hose and black orthopedic shoes. She appeared to be clean, but a distinct musty cloud of oldness hung over her. She wore a great deal of dark red lipstick for a woman her age. The effect of the lipstick was that her mouth looked somehow disconnected from her person and seemed unnaturally young.

"I'm Old Margaret," she said.

"I'm—"

She interrupted me. "I already know who you are."

"Are you related to Maggie?" I asked.

"I should say so." She laughed.

I watched her mouth. "I meant, *how* are you related to Maggie?"

"I should really ask how you're related to her."

"Come again?"

"What did you mean when you tied that string around her finger?"

"I meant . . . ," I began. "She told you about that?"

"I'm only teasing, of course." She smiled, which was only slightly horrifying. "Would you mind terribly if I had a smoke?"

I shook my head.

"Don't tell anyone," she said.

Old Margaret opened the window and lit her cigarette. "Greta would have made you light it for her. She was so old-fashioned, but I'm not. Of course, I wouldn't mind if you'd light it for me, it is gentlemanly, but seeing as you're somewhat incapacitated, we must make concessions."

Whoever Greta was, I thought. Would Maggie be like this at one hundred?

"No," Old Margaret answered, "she doesn't smoke. I started smoking when I was thirteen. I was very advanced. In those days, we didn't worry about cancer or emphysema or all that nonsense. Also, I'm only seventy-seven. But I can see how you might think I was older. We're only experts at determining the ages we are, after all. Everyone else just looks old or young, and in a way, everyone older or younger than ourselves ceases to be quite human."

Had I spoken out loud?

"I'm a mind reader," she replied. "It was a gift I acquired after the change. That, and the ability to smell people's emotions. I think that might be part of the same gift, actually." She sniffed the air. "You smell injured, but I suppose that's a little obvious. Does your leg hurt?"

"Not too much. It's uncomfortable more than anything."

"Well, they have you on a lot of painkillers. It'll hurt soon enough. I've had two hip replacement surgeries, so I know of what I speak." She knocked on my cast. "You'll have to be in bed for at least two weeks. That's what Maggie said. I hope it won't be too boring for you with only us spinsters to amuse you."

"Who are you, anyway?"

"Old Margaret," she repeated, as if I were very slow indeed.

"Was Maggie named for you?"

"Was Maggie named for me?" She paused. "Yes, I suppose she was."

"Are you Maggie's grandmother?"

"Aren't I too young to be Maggie's grandmother?"

"No," I answered slowly, "no, not really."

Old Margaret sighed. "I suppose I am Maggie's grandmother then. How awful!"

Old Margaret was clearly somewhat senile.

"I am not senile," she said, "and it's very rude of you to even say that."

"I didn't say it," I protested. "I thought it."

"Sometimes I can't tell the difference. In that case, concessions must be made. If you had actually said it, it would have hurt me enormously, but as you only thought it, it just stings a bit."

I didn't really see what difference it made in either case.

"Well," she said, "if you had said it aloud, you would have meant to hurt me. And we can't always control what we think. For example, I know you thought I smelled musty when I first came in the room. And that might have hurt my feelings, too, but who wants to spend her whole life offended?"

"I'm sorry."

"It's mothballs by the way. Ever since I turned sixty-five, I've had an enormous moth problem that I never had before then. Why do you think that is?"

"I don't know."

"Why don't young people ever have problems with moths?" she asked. "Moths are the bedfellows of the aged, wouldn't you agree?"

"If you don't mind, I'm feeling sort of tired," I said.

"Of course you are, dear," she said. "How completely inconsiderate of me." She put out her cigarette and hobbled toward the door. The two hip replacements had left her with a pronounced limp.

"Who else lives here?" I asked.

"Well, there's Me, Marge, Mia, and May. And now Maggie's back, too. You probably won't see much of May, as she prefers to be out of doors. And there used to be one more, too, but she's gone, gone, never to return, gone."

"And these are Maggie's"—I tried to remember—"aunts?"

"Oh yes," she said. "Or in all cases, something very like. I'm sorry if I've tired you with all my chatter. Do you know I was considered very quiet when I was a girl? So it's strange that now that I'm older, I find I have so much to say."

She closed the door very gently. In fact, the shutting of the door seemed to last about ten minutes. I tell you, Jane, it would have been preferable if she had slammed it.

Minutes or hours or days later (when you are heavily medicated, distinctions in time are harder to determine), I awoke to find Maggie curled up next to me like a cat. She had a black eye but, other than that, appeared undamaged.

"When did you come in here?" I asked.

"A while ago. I didn't want to wake you." She looked at my leg and started to cry. "I'm sorry I fell asleep. You probably think I'm the worst driver in the whole entire world." She tugged at the string, which was retied around her finger.

"You were tired." There is never any point in being retributive, especially with women who are self-retributive by nature. "I should have been wearing my seat belt."

"I am the worst driver in the whole entire world. You can admit it."

"No—"

"Admit it!" she demanded.

"You may very well be the worst driver in the whole entire world, but not having met all the other drivers in the world, I can't confirm this for sure. You did manage to save the car and yourself from any serious injury. If you hadn't reacted so quickly when you did wake up, we both might have died."

"I am such a fucking mess. I am a fucking disaster. I am a goddamn plague is what I am."

"Will it make you feel better if I admit you are the worst driver I know?"

"Yes!" And suddenly, she laughed. That's how it was with Maggie. From laughter to tears in less than a second. She *loved* (in italics) or she *hated* (in italics). She was emotionally reckless. While it was thrilling for me to watch, I suspect it was rather hard for her to *live* that way.

My room was very small, so in the beginning, they came to see me one at a time. In addition to Maggie and Old Margaret, I know I was visited by Marge and Mia. Owing to a generous supply of painkillers, the specifics of these encounters remain somewhat hazy. [Only the littlest one, May, who I assumed at the time was Maggie's cousin or niece, never appeared during my horizontal period. May was seven at the time, twice as old as you were when we met.] I don't really remember being formally introduced to Marge, Mia, or May. It was like I was born knowing them.

I shall describe them for you, Jane, though I'm not sure these impressions truly constitute first impressions. I am told by Bess that knowing what a person looks like and their general character is important to readers and especially girls.

After Old Margaret, the next oldest was Marge. She was in her fifties and rather stout. Her hair was reddish at the ends and white at the crown and too long for a woman her age. She wore an eye patch over her left eye. The patch had a green eye painted on it, which was incredibly creepy. She seemed to loathe me from the moment she met me. She asked me a lot about my work, which is normally a sure sign that someone hates you. Also, I knew she hated men because early in our relationship she told me so. "I hate men," Marge said, "and you oughtn't take it personally."

Mia was seventeen and wanted nothing to do

with me. Through an elaborate display of eye rolling and scowling, she made it clear that her visits were not by choice. (Perversely, I tried to flirt with her a bit.) She wore her dark red hair so that it covered most of her face. She dressed all in black and her nails were always painted to match in shades of black or blood red. She wore an excess of dark eye makeup that didn't suit her complexion at all. She was constantly writing or drawing something in a black book, which no one was allowed to see.

May was seven and rarely seen indoors. Consequently, she was dirty and tan. Indeed, it was hard to say where the dirt began and the tan ended. She wore her hair in two pigtails. Her knees were in a state of constant excoriation. She had a yo-yo. She was missing her two front teeth. If you asked her a question, her usual response was to giggle and run away.

So, including Maggie, there were five women living in Margarettown that summer. You might ask yourself, Did anyone else live there? The answer is no and not really. No, in that Margarettown was a ghost town and these women cultivated their isolation. Not really, in that it wouldn't have mattered to me if other people had been there. In a way, whoever you know in a certain place defines that place for you.

3.

After a week, I was out of traction and able to move around on crutches. My first night about, I had dinner with the five women of Margarettown.

Old Margaret sat at one end of the table, and Marge at the other. Mia sat on Old Margaret's left, and Maggie to Old Margaret's right. I sat next to Maggie, and May sat across from me.

The food was unmemorable. None of the women seemed to have acquired much in the way of culinary skills.

Seventeen-year-old Mia asked with a scowl, "What's that dirty string around your finger, Maggie?"

Maggie covered her hand. "It's to remind me of something," she said.

"You look like a crazy person," Mia said. She lowered her voice. "Like Greta."

Old Margaret tried to change the subject. "Did you know that our little town has an echo?"

"Yes, we heard it before we crashed."

"An echo makes for very good company," Old Margaret said. "Whenever I'm lonely, I always try to find one to talk to. They're much better than mirrors. Mirrors say nasty things about you. Echoes are far more supportive. They think whatever you say is completely brilliant."

"So, you're Maggie's grandmother," I said to Old Margaret. "And the rest of you all are Maggie's, um, aunts?"

May giggled.

"Well, obviously not you," I said to May.

"I should have been more clear before," Maggie said. "Marge is my only aunt."

Marge laughed.

"And May is my cousin. And Mia is my sister," Maggie finished.

"Hey, *Sis*," Mia said.

"You and Mia and May all look a lot alike," I observed.

"You don't think *I* look like Maggie?" Marge asked wickedly. "*I* think I look very much like Maggie actually."

I considered Marge. She really looked nothing like Maggie. Aside from the eye patch and frizzy hair, she was overweight and thirty years older. It was more than that, though. Marge's one exposed eye was black and angry. No matter how old Maggie got, her eyes (eye?) could never look like that. In a way, Maggie looked more like Old Margaret, who was almost eighty.

"I don't really see a resemblance," I admitted.

Marge snorted. "Give it time; you will."

"So, what do you do for a living?" Old Margaret asked me.

"He's an academic," Maggie answered for me. "We met at U."

"Maggie, you aren't sleeping with your teacher, are you?" Mia asked. "Gross."

"I was only a teaching assistant," I corrected her.

"Like that really makes a difference. It's still incredibly gross and probably unethical," Mia replied.

"What's your field?" Marge asked me.

"Philosophy," I replied.

"A philosopher! Good one, Mag," Mia said in a tone I can only assume was sarcastic.

Marge snorted. "We slept with a philosopher once before. It was a disaster."

I didn't completely understand her use of the term "we."

Old Margaret laughed the same laugh as Maggie. "He was the one who was awful in bed, wasn't he? You can't philosophize your way to being good in bed, now can you, young man?"

Marge snorted again. This time, an appreciative one. She had several different kinds of snorts.

I was starting to find these five women completely overwhelming.

"Why are you always so attracted to unsuitable men?" Marge asked Maggie. "Would it be so hard to find an investment banker or a dermatologist or a lawyer? Someone who will actually love us and provide for us when we're old."

"Hey, remember when she fell in love with that married guy!" Mia asked.

"He wasn't married," Maggie defended herself. "He was engaged."

"Big difference." Mia rolled her eyes. Those eyes were in a perpetual state of rolling.

"Besides which, that wasn't me anyway," Maggie said.

"Yes, it was," Mia insisted.

"It was Greta," May quietly volunteered.

At the mention of that name, the table grew very quiet.

"You're right, May; it *was* Greta," Marge said. "Poor Greta."

Old Margaret lifted her water glass. "To Greta. Wherever she may be!"

The others raised their glasses. "To Greta," they chorused.

"Who's Greta?" I asked.

"Do you know? We should all sign your cast," Old Margaret said after a moment.

"You really don't have to."

"No, that's the only good thing about breaking a leg," Old Margaret insisted. "Mia's quite the artist, you know. I'm sure she could come up with something lovely."

"Yeah, I really want to spend a lot of time decorating the old guy's cast," Mia said. She shook her head in disgust and left the table.

"May, it's your night to clear," Marge instructed.

May nodded. She didn't say much, but for my money, that made her the most pleasant of the group.

"Hey, I'm only thirty-one," I said. Frankly, my protest was too late. Everyone was already leaving. As I could not yet maneuver quickly, I was left sitting alone.

[In reading this over, I fear I have not accurately conveyed what that dinner was like. The limitations of prose (or at least my prose) do not express the

way the women constantly overlapped and interrupted one another. Although I have reduced it to
one main conversational thread, in point of fact,
several conversations were occurring simultane-
ously. I might liken the effect to an auction in a very
echoey room.]

4.

The first time Maggie and I had sex at Margaron was about two weeks after that dinner. It coincided with the first day I could make it up the stairs to Maggie's bedroom.

The kind of sex you have in a woman's girlhood home is of a charming and slightly disturbing nature. One, you have to be quiet, which lends the whole event an aura of the forbidden. Two, there is all this evidence that she lived a life before you even existed: letters and yearbooks and ancient corsages and cheerleading skirts. And three, if the room still retains too much of its childhood decor, one can feel a bit like one is having sex with a child. In Maggie's room, the carpet had faded pink roses on it. She had a lamp that looked like a circus tent. The lamp threw moon and star shadows around the room. Her bed was a twin. In those days, twin beds followed us everywhere.

Maggie was never the most vocal during sex, but

the ancient box springs of the twin were comically squeaky. The bed sounded like a very old woman trying to make it up a mountain. Consequently, I'm pretty sure the whole household must have heard us. (Except, of course, for Old Margaret, who was going deaf.) A rhythmic banging accompanied our denouement. Maggie later claimed it was the pipes, but I knew it was Marge. And, in a way, it was almost like I was fucking Marge, too. I even found myself picturing Marge's pinched face in place of Maggie's. Even after we were done, I found I was still thinking of Marge.

"Say, Maggie? The name Marge can also be a nickname for Margaret, can't it?"

"I suppose," she said. "So?"

"Well, I was wondering if your aunt Marge's name is Margaret, too?"

She rolled away from me. "Mmm, I guess so."

"And the name May? Isn't that also short for Margaret?"

"It could be."

"And the name Mia?"

"Mmm hmm."

"So counting you and Old Margaret, are all five of you really called Margaret?"

"Why? Does it matter?"

"And," I continued, "do *all* of you have the last name Towne?"

"I don't see why you're getting so excited."

"It's just one of those things that would be nice to know."

"I'm sorry," she said.

"It's just one of those things that one appreciates being brought to one's attention."

"I said I was sorry, although I don't see how it matters," she said.

"Well, why didn't you mention it before?"

Maggie sighed. "I thought you knew."

She got up to go to the bathroom. I had to go, too, but in my condition, it seemed like too much bother. Upon her return, I asked her, "But why are you all called Margaret?"

"Because we are."

"But isn't it, um, odd?" I persisted.

"To tell you the truth, I've never thought much about it. As long as I can remember, it's always been that way, so it doesn't seem at all odd to me."

"But—"

"Do you know what I've always liked about you?" she asked. "I like that you don't ask me a lot of questions about every last little thing. I like that you don't think that knowing everything about me is some prerequisite to sleeping together or paying for my dinner or anything else. Believe it or not, I actually like that we don't know everything about each other."

She turned off the moon and stars, and rolled away from me.

"Maggie," I began again.

"What?" She looked at me, and her face was more Marge than I had ever seen it. For the first time, I could really see the resemblance.

"Nothing."

She tossed and turned several more times before jumping out of bed. "I really can't get comfortable. I should probably sleep downstairs anyway," she said. And then in a softer voice, "You probably need more room for your leg."

I wanted to protest, but I didn't have the energy. Besides, she was probably right. And so, she kissed me and left.

That night, I dreamed I was having sex with Maggie, only her face kept slipping off like a mask. And underneath the mask was Marge.

5.

The name Margaret derives from the Greek word *margaron*, which means pearl. The name came to English by way of the Latin name Margarita and the Old French name Marguerite. Margaret has more nicknames than any other female name in the English language. In addition to Mia, Maggie, and May, others include Grete, Margitta, Gretta, Madge, Maggy, Maisey, Maisie, Mamie, Marg, Margie, Margorie, Margy, Marjie, Meg, Megan, Meggi, Meggie, Meggy, Metta, Peg, Peggie, Peggy, Em, and Marga. The name also has four alternate spellings (Margarett, Margarit, Margret, and Margeret) and twenty-eight alternate English forms (Grethe, Reeree, Marit, Magaret, Makaleka, Maragaret, Maragret, Maret, Margaretta, Margarette, Margarite, Margaritta, Margart, Margene, Margerete, Margert, Margery, Marget, Margrete, Margrett, Marguerita, Marguerite, Margueritte, Marjorie, Marjory, Markita, Marquerite, and Maretta). The name Margaret has equivalents in many lan-

guages: in Bulgarian, Croatian, German, and Ser-
bian, Margareta; in Czech, Marka or Marketa; in
Danish, Margrethe or Margit; in Dutch, Margriet;
in Finnish, Marketta or Marjatta; in German, Margret, Margarethe, Margitta, or Margarete; in Hungar-
ian, Margarta; in Italian, Margherita; in Norwegian
and Swedish, Margit; in Polish, Margarita or Mal-
gorzata; in Romanian, Spanish, and Russian, Margarita; in Gaelic, Mairead; and in Welsh, Mared or
Marged. Someone once called Margaret "the national
Scottish name" but I do not know who nor do I
know what led the person to make this pronounce-
ment. The name ranked ninth in popularity for all
female names in the 1990 U.S. Census.

Having so many forms, it is easy to mock the Margarets of the world. Teasing nicknames include the following: Mugrat, Mugger, Pegasus, Marg A Rat, Magpie,
Large Marge, Margarine, Margy Pargy, Megger,
Meggy Weggy, Mug Wump, May Zit, Peglit, and Mag-
got. I am sure there are many, many others. Children
are at their most industrious when inventing ways to
torment one another.

Maggie liked to say that naming a daughter Margaret was as good as not naming her at all.

The Margarets each signed my cast in a different color. Old Margaret signed in red, Marge in yellow, Maggie in blue, and May in pink. May could only print her first name, MAY, and Mia declined to sign at all.

I was staring at my leg one night (there was really nothing to do that summer) when I noticed how similar all three signatures were. Old Margaret's was a bit shaky perhaps, but aside from that, the three signatures were practically identical.

Margaret Towne in red on my calf.

Margaret Towne in yellow on my ankle.

Margaret Towne in blue on my thigh.

And at that moment, an idea began to rumble about in my head, an idea too absurd to be plausible. Yet, it seemed possible based on the following evidence:

- Five women named Margaret Towne living in one house.
- Margaret Towne in red; Margaret Towne in yellow; Margaret Towne in blue.
- Maggie in the gap claiming she was cursed.

Maybe you have suspected it for some time, Jane?

✧

So, I did what any good hero would do. I decided to save Maggie. I packed suitcases for both of us and convinced her to run away. She wasn't hard to persuade actually. Ingrained in the Margaret character was the instinct to run.

We left in the middle of the night. In retrospect, maybe this was not quite courageous or even very wise. Maybe if I had confronted the other Margarets right then and there, it would have turned out better for everyone. Maybe, but ingrained in *my* character was the instinct to avoid confrontation, especially with women.

Despite any misgivings I may have had about her abilities, Maggie had to drive Jacques's convertible on account of my leg. We had only just passed over the Margarettown bridge when Maggie slammed on the brakes and turned off the engine.

"What is it?" I asked her.

"We're cursed," Maggie said. "We're doomed."

"We're fine," I assured her. "We'll leave here. We'll live happily ever after."

"We're not. We can't." She paused. "We won't."

"Why?"

"Those women—"

I interrupted her. "Oh, forget your sisters! Who cares about your sisters?"

"Those women aren't my sisters," she said. "You know very well they aren't my sisters. I told you before they weren't my sisters."

I paused. "Well, who are they, Maggie?"

"It's like I said, we're cursed," she repeated miserably.

"Stop saying that. Isn't *cursed* putting things a tad strongly?"

"I mean it in the literal sense. I am a woman who is cursed. We are women who have been cursed." She paused. "When a normal woman gets older, she leaves no evidence. Every few years, I leave an entire person."

"I know," I said. And on some level, I suppose I did.

Her eyes were hard. "If you know, then you should also know that driving away won't solve anything. They follow me. They find me. They're always with me."

"But Maggie—"

"I'm not even the first Margaret. I'm not the original; you only see me as the original, because I'm the first one you met. Old Margaret is the first, and I'm actually the fourth. Just one of many. Somewhere after Mia and before Greta."

"But how can you be the fourth? That doesn't make any—"

She interrupted me. "Because I'm a monster," she said, "and no one will ever love me."

"I already love you."

"But can you love Marge? You loathe Marge and she's me, too. And Mia's impossible! And Old Margaret's . . . *old*! She's so old, N.! And May is completely childish."

"Indeed, she is a child," I pointed out.

"Unless you love all of us, you don't really love any of us," she said.

"But in a way, those women aren't you," I pointed out. "They're like you, but they're completely separate from you, right? It's quirky and a bit strange, yes. But does it really make a difference in the long run anyway?"

Maggie shook her head. "I have to go back. I don't expect you to come with me, N. I don't expect you to take on all of this. We haven't really known each other for very long. And it's too much to ask of anyone. You aren't the first either." She untied the string from around her finger and set it on the dashboard. "I pretended this was more than a string," she said, "but it may have been only a string after all."

"Maggie," I said, "I can't leave without you. I can't drive, but even if I could, I don't want to."

"Call your sister. She'll drive you home. You have a dissertation to get back to anyway."

"Nothing has changed," I told her. "We can still go back to Boston, live in my basement, order bad takeout." I longed for Maggie in my basement. What I had not realized at the time was that those months in the basement had been happiness, or something very like it.

"I just can't leave them right now," she said.

"I love you," I told her.

"Love." Maggie snorted like Marge. "Under these conditions, I'm afraid it would be difficult to love anyone."

Maggie turned the car back on, and we drove back to Margaron. I decided I would go without her. Not because I necessarily wanted to, but because she told me to.

Why does anyone ever fall in love with anyone? Is it the dimple in a plump elbow? Is it a glint in the eye? When you fall in love with one woman, are you actually falling in love with a different woman entirely? A prior woman who somehow set the stage for this woman?

Who the hell knows?

Before your mother, my heart was little more than a seed, Jane. A wiggly, gelatinous nothing, rather like a solitary sperm.

6.

Aside from my mother and for a very brief time my sister, my first real love was my uncle Jacques's mistress, Miranda. She was also the first woman I slept with, although this didn't happen until I was nearly sixteen. We slept together off and on until I graduated from college.

Once, after intercourse, I asked Miranda if she was offended that Jacques never asked her to marry him.

"Little man," she said, "I would absolutely loathe being his wife. Jack is a terrible husband and a wonderful lover." Miranda was the only one who could get away with calling him Jack.

Jacques was probably more devoted to Miranda than he was to any of his wives. Indeed, their relationship lasted from wives two through four. (It ended only because Miranda died at the age of forty-four.)

I remember the day I met Miranda. In a way, it was very like the day I met your mother.

I was nine. I had wandered into Jacques's bedroom to ask him to sign a permission slip and I
found Miranda, in dishabille except for a string of
pearls, lying on Jacques's massive mahogany bed.
She made no attempt to cover herself. She was the
first woman I had ever seen naked aside from my
mother and, of course, my sister. [Question: in
those early days, is there a link between seeing a
woman naked and falling in love with her?]

"What is it you want?" Miranda asked. I was never
able to identify her accent. Suffice it to say, she
sounded rich and foreign.

"I was looking for Jacques," I said. I tried to stop
myself from staring at her breasts.

"He is not here," she said. "May I help you?"

I held out my permission slip meekly. "I just
needed him to sign this. It's for a school trip."

"Where is the trip?" she demanded.

The trip was to the Seaquarium, but the thought
of saying the word "Seaquarium" to this naked woman
was more than I could bear. I wanted to be going
somewhere glamorous, somewhere that would
impress her. In sixth grade (I was only in fourth),
they went to Sturbridge Village, so that's what I
answered. "Sturbridge Village."

"Sturbridge Village?" She was incredulous. "Do you mean with the log cabins and the cotton loom and the oxen?"

"Yes," I said.

"I have never been there. It sounds dreadful." She gestured grandly toward me. "Bring me your paper. I will forge Jack's signature for you."

"Can you do that?" I asked.

"Please! I do it all the time," she said.

Despite any qualms I might have had about the ethics of her offer, I brought her the paper and handed her a pen. She signed his name in a practiced manner. "So you know, little man, it says here that you are going to the Seaquarium."

Oh, the humiliation! My ears burned to hear her say "Seaquarium"! "It's a mistake," I lied desperately, "a stupid, stupid mistake."

She shrugged, tossing her long red hair over her shoulders. "In any case, the Seaquarium seems a much better way to pass an afternoon than Sturbridge Village," she said.

I stopped *not* looking at her breasts for a moment in order to look in her eyes. I saw amusement and understanding there, and I was in love. At that age (or any age for that matter), our hearts are simple enough.

"You're very pretty," I told her.

"Little man," she said, "so you know, I cannot sleep with you at least until you have passed through puberty."

I nodded and made a mental note.

Miranda had red hair like Margaret, and the two women did share a certain resemblance. You may ask yourself, was Miranda the Margaret before Margaret? Had there been no Miranda, would there be no Margaret? Was I cursed to love this woman? Was I destined? When it comes down to it, are curses and destiny really the same things?

Who the hell knows?

Before your mother, my heart was a seed, Jane. A funny little nothing, rather like a lone sperm.

7.

Although I considered calling Bess to come and get me, I ultimately decided against it. At that particular moment, I wasn't up to dealing with her love and concern. So instead, I called a person who didn't particularly love me, who already thought I was an asshole, but who would still be obligated to come for me anyway. I called my uncle Jacques. I know I said before that he was dead, but what I really meant to say was that he was mostly dead. That is to say, Uncle Jacques was dead whenever it was convenient to me. From time to time, it became necessary to resurrect him, however.

In those days, Uncle Jacques had just divorced his fifth wife and was living on a houseboat in a variety of locations.

I dialed his number.

"Yes?" Uncle Jacques said in his stupid Belgian accent. "What is it you need?"

"I need you to come and get me. I'm in a town in upstate New York."

"Upstate New York? No one should ever go there—it is a toilet!" Uncle Jacques said. "Why can you not drive yourself or fly?"

"I've been injured," I said. "I've broken my leg and I need someone else to drive me."

Uncle Jacques found this enormously funny for some reason. "Oh ho ho. Were you skiing?"

"No," I answered.

"Were you country line dancing?"

"No."

"Were you having ze sex?"

"No."

"Were you—"

"For Christ's sake, Jacques. I was in a car accident."

"Are you completely okeydokey?"

"No. I broke my leg," I repeated.

"Why can you not call your sister, Elizabeth?" Uncle Jacques asked.

"Bess is saving the rainforests this summer."

"Okeydokey, I will be there in three weeks," Uncle Jacques said.

"Can't you come any sooner?"

"No. I am in Tahiti. This is how long it takes to return by ze boat. I call you when I get to ze States. Ciao!" And then Uncle Jacques hung up the phone.

Marge had been listening to my entire conversation. "You're leaving us," she said gleefully. "I can't say it surprises me much."

"Hey, Marge," I retorted, "how'd you lose that eye?"

She smiled wickedly. "Maggie stabbed me. She claimed she only wanted to cut my hair, but I knew better."

"Why would Maggie want to stab you?" I asked.

"It was the last time one of you came around." Marge snorted. "I told her it wouldn't last, and it didn't. As usual, I was right. Not that anyone ever listens to Marge."

The thought that my Maggie could turn into this bitter woman seemed impossible. It was enough to make me glad I was leaving.

8.

While I waited for Jacques to arrive from Tahiti, relations between Maggie and me were strained. And yet, I did not find my time in Margarettown completely unpleasant.

That summer was a bit like retirement. I took walks; I read books; I rested; I healed. It was boring, yes, but it is remarkable how closely boredom and happiness can resemble each other.

It was nicest to walk with Old Margaret. Having had two hip replacement surgeries, she didn't move much faster than me. On those walks, she didn't ask much of me either. Maybe she didn't need to, since she could read all my thoughts anyway. In any case, she was perfectly willing to do all the talking.

"I'm the oldest Margaret Towne and the first," Old Margaret said. "I was born in 19__, right here in this house.

"The second Margaret was May. She appeared

right before my seventh birthday. One day, she just came in for dinner. As she looked like my twin, no one wanted to tell her to leave. Obviously, the appearance of a second me gave my mother quite a shock. My father drank a bit in those days and thought my mother might be trying to fool with him. He said, 'I can't remember. Did we have twins?' My mother began to sob. Father assumed that my mother's sobs were in anger at his failure to remember that I was a twin, and from that day forward, he never drank again.

"The oddest thing about May, and indeed all the Margarets after me, was that they never aged. While I continued to get older, they always stayed exactly the age they were when they had first arrived. It always seemed to me that they *should* age, but of course, I've never had anything with which to compare it.

"When I was seventeen, Mia showed up in the middle of a date I was having with a boy named Michael Levy. I had gone to the bathroom to powder my nose. When I returned, I found Mia at the table, and she and Mike were kissing. (She was always more advanced than me sexually.) I decided not to interrupt them, but I broke up with him the following week. If he couldn't tell the difference

between me and another me, I wanted nothing more
to do with him. He didn't really care, of course, as he
was more interested in my new 'cousin' (that was
what we called her) from out of town.

"When I was twenty-five, both my parents were
killed in an automobile accident. Maggie arrived that
same year, 19__. Mia hated when Maggie arrived,
because Maggie was definitely the prettiest one."

I agreed that she was.

"I'm delightful at that age, aren't I? I'm always the
prettiest from twenty-five to thirty-five. Although I
was very pretty in my teens, there was a certain
roundness to my face that was retained until my
mid-twenties. By the time I was twenty-five, though,
the roundness was gone, and I was at my loveliest. I
do have one final burst of beauty around forty however." Old Margaret sighed at the thought of it.

"The year I was thirty-five, Greta arrived. You
will never meet Greta because she killed herself the
year I was thirty-nine. We call her the Lost Margaret.
It was a very sad time. After Greta, there was only
one other Margaret and that was Marge, who arrived
when I was fifty-two, the same year I began menopause. And the last twenty-five years have been
rather quiet, I suppose. I am told I haven't changed

much during this time, which may very well be why no other Margarets have appeared."

"If it isn't too rude to ask, how did the Lost Margaret kill herself?" I asked.

"Pills and then she drowned herself," Old Margaret said. "Poor Greta, she was always such a completist. I suppose I'm the same way."

Old Margaret patted me on the hand. Her knuckles were distorted from arthritis and her hands were covered in liver spots. "I like you, young man," she said, "and it is easy to see why Maggie likes you, too."

I was very fond of Old Margaret, as well. [I wish you had met her, Jane.]

One day, I asked Old Margaret why she thought Margarettown was the way it was.

Her theory was rambling, romantic, and completely confusing: "Father was dying, but he wanted to be sure his daughter would find true love, a love for all time. He knew that only a man who could appreciate his daughter across many ages would truly be worthy. So Father got his spinster sister Sarah, who was a witch of some reputation in the region, to place an enchantment on his newborn daughter. The enchantment would split her into multiple ages until she found true love. When the daughter found true love, the spell would be broken, and she would become one again." Old Margaret had said all that without pausing for breath. "Sadly," Old Margaret confessed, "true love is somewhat harder to come by than Father thought." And then Old Margaret said, "I just made all that up, of course." She laughed, as did I.

"Maggie calls it a curse," I said.

Old Margaret rolled her eyes, looking a bit like Mia when she did that. "That's youth for you," she said. "I don't really see it as a *curse* at all. It's been a blessing, really. All these years, I've always had myself for company and I make for very nice company indeed."

Old Margaret and I were sitting on the front lawn of Margaron. Marge poked her head out from the kitchen. "I tell you, it's not so damn extraordinary as you make it out to be. I've lived a lot longer than you, and I tell you, you won't find a woman in the world that doesn't have a couple other women inside her." She also said that Maggie was a "damn fool" and I shouldn't listen to anything that "damn fool woman" said.

From her treehouse, May overheard us, too. She looked down from the treehouse with wide eyes. "What's a *curse*?" she said.

Maggie was in the porch swing, reading a book. She gave us a dirty look and called to May, "There's no *curse*, darling. Don't worry about it."

"Okay," May replied sweetly.

"May doesn't know?" I asked Maggie that night in bed. I'm not sure why we were still sleeping together at this point. I suppose it was more out of habit than anything. Not to mention, I couldn't sleep without her.

"Why should she?" Maggie asked. "What good has knowing ever done any of us? She probably does know anyway, but if she prefers to pretend she doesn't, who are any of us to say differently?"

"Don't you ever wonder why you're like this?" I asked.

"I don't ask why," she said. "It is what it is."

"Can I help you?" I asked her.

"I doubt it," she said. "When is your uncle coming?"

"Soon," I replied. "Very soon."

There was only one bathroom at Margaron. Living with five women, I found this situation somewhat untenable. (Sharing a bathroom with just one woman can be fairly untenable.) Marge had told me there was a nonoperational toilet on the third floor. "Maybe you can fix it," she said with a laugh. Based on her tone, I knew it wasn't likely. Still, when I could make it up the three flights of stairs with relative ease, I decided to investigate the second bathroom.

The third floor had seven doors and was basically used as an attic. I quickly located the bathroom, which was the first door next to the stairs. The toilet was, indeed, not working and, from what I could tell, would probably never work again. Apparently, it had not been working so long, someone had decided to use it as a planter. Red and white tulips bloomed from the bowl.

As I was up there already (and going down stairs was even harder than going up for me), I decided to

see what else was on the third floor. Behind the second door, I found a piano and a music stand.
Behind the third door, shelves and shelves of school
textbooks. Behind the fourth door, a room that
looked just like a dorm room (though not the one
that I had found her in that first night). Behind the
fifth door, a rack of what looked like costumes.
Behind the sixth door, six paintings, all portraits
(possibly self-portraits) of Margaret at different
ages. The last door, the seventh, was locked.

I tried to force it open, but I couldn't. Bright
light poured out from the crack under the door.
(Maybe I imagined this light?) I peeked through the
keyhole, but I couldn't make anything out.

Later that night, I asked Maggie about the seventh room.

"What's in the locked room?" I asked her.

"Oh," she said casually, "it's nothing very interesting. Just storage. A bunch of stuff no one needs
anymore anyway."

"So, why is it locked?"

"It's an accident really. At some point, Greta had
the key and it went . . ." She gestured over her shoul-
der, and her watch slipped down her wrist. I noticed
a faint vertical scar that I had never seen before.

"Maggie," I said, "have you always had that?"

"Yes," she said. "Well, not always, but as long as you've known me."

"What's it from?"

"An experiment that didn't work out," she said.

"It looks like a serious experiment," I said.

She shook her head and said nothing.

"It's strange I never noticed it before," I said.

Still she said nothing. I continued to try to get Maggie to tell me about her "experiment." All she would say was "it's nothing very interesting."

So I kissed her scar, and we left it at that.

10.

The third Margaret, Mia, wanted to be a painter. (The decision to major in Art History at U had come as a major disappointment to her.) She was constantly sketching or painting or doodling, although she wouldn't let anyone see the results. Mia had been sullen toward me since my arrival. Consequently, I was surprised when she said she wanted to draw me. I later learned that Old Margaret had suggested it.

Mia said she wanted to set up her easel by the river, about fifty yards from the bridge where the accident had been. By this time, I was getting around all right on my crutches and I was glad to be out of that house.

"I've thought about what my ideal man is like, and frankly, he's not like you," Mia said. "For one, you're old."

"Not compared to Maggie, I'm not."

"I just mean, he comes in around twenty-five, tops. And for two, you don't play cello."

"Am I supposed to?"

"Well, it wouldn't hurt," she said. "And if you aren't going to play cello, you ought to, at the very least, be in a band. And he has a dog, a big yellow one. You don't have a dog, do you?"

I shook my head.

"And his forearms are bigger than yours. And you know those bulging veins some men get in their hands? Well, he has those, too." Mia sighed. "You're not bad-looking if you go for that thin, useless look. I just can't believe you're Maggie's type, though."

"If you were eight years older, I'd be your type, too, you know," I said.

"I know. It's completely depressing."

I laughed. "So, you could never see yourself with me?"

She shook her head. "Not really, but in a way, it shouldn't matter to you. You should worry more about the older Margarets anyway. May and I, we're the past, we're what Maggie has already been."

"Well, Marge doesn't seem to like me much either."

"She doesn't like anyone. She doesn't like me or Maggie or May." Mia shrugged. "I think she finds us all somewhat disappointing. I find her somewhat disappointing myself."

"I'm in love with Maggie, you know."

"I know you are. It's obvious."

"Is it?"

"Yeah, totally. Personally, I could never love you, not that way." She stopped speaking abruptly and looked at me. "Are you going to marry her?"

"I'm not sure," I said.

"You really ought to know one way or the other," Mia said, sounding exactly like Bess.

"So I'm told."

She sketched in silence for about twenty minutes. Suddenly, she smiled. "Do you know? Your nose is really rather nice."

"Thanks."

"I think I'll just draw your nose, if that's okay. It's the best part of your face." She ripped off the first sheet and crumpled it up.

Mia threw her whole self into drawing my nose. She was completely engaged in it. Her eyes burned brightly, and her limbs flew every which way. Before long, it was dusk, and we had to go inside.

I was glad for the opportunity to watch her. To be able to see the woman you love as a teenager—all long legs and odd passions and curious notions— and know that she will grow into another woman entirely. Even though this girl could never love me, it was incredibly easy to fall in love with her all the same. Maggie who once was Mia who once was May.

When we had reached Margaron again, I said to her, "You're lovely, you know."

She lowered her head, but I could tell she was pleased. "I'm all right."

"No, you're lovely. You just don't know it yet."

"Would you like to see your nose?"

I nodded. She opened her sketch book and showed her drawing to me.

"It's a good nose," I told her. And it was. Although I must admit that it was somewhat horrifying to see any one part of myself considered to that extent.

"I like noses," she said. "They're the only part of the face that occurs without repetition. Everything else has a double: two eyes, two eyebrows, two lips, two ears."

"Noses have two holes," I pointed out.

She dismissed me. "Holes don't count."

I shook her hand. It was smaller than Maggie's, bony, the paw of a girl. I also noticed that she bit her nails.

"I'll sign your cast now," she said. She took a magic marker out of her pocket and bent over to work. I couldn't see what she had done until she was finished: it was a doodle of a frog wearing a crown, and underneath that, her signature.

"It's the frog prince," she said.

"I know. It's very good."

"Do you know the story of the frog prince?" she asked me.

"A gal kisses a frog and he turns into a prince, or some such."

"That's the nice version," Mia told me. "In the real version, the frog threatens the girl because she doesn't want to kiss him. I mean, he is a frog. So she chucks him as hard as she can against a wall, and then he becomes a prince. She basically beats the prince out of him."

"Nice story," I said. "Think of all those poor girls out there kissing frogs when it isn't ever going to make a damn bit of difference."

Maggie came out of the house then. She looked at Mia's handiwork. "Interesting," she said.

Mia rolled her eyes at Maggie and then she went inside.

Maggie and I sat down in the porch swing. With my cast, getting in the swing was more difficult than it sounds, and she had to help me.

"You were adorable at seventeen," I told her.

Maggie laughed. "I was awful. I was arrogant and scared and judgmental and basically, I hated myself. To be honest, I almost find her painful to be around."

"I repeat, you were adorable."

"My legs *were* really thin then," she conceded.

II.

Before you, Jane, I never really liked children much. I mean I positively adored them in the abstract, with their pink cheeks and their silky hair. However, the thought of spending any extended time with a specific, concrete child was distinctly unappealing.

Children are generally miserable and cruel people. And for good reason. For one, they are very short, and for two, childhood is a generally miserable time, but older people are always insisting children should be happier than they are.

Perhaps it's because Bess and I were raised by Uncle Jacques, who also did not like children much. Uncle Jacques also hated cats, and I, too, hate cats.

So although seven-year-old May seemed nice enough, I had, for the most part, avoided her. It was easy to avoid her, as I'm pretty sure she was avoiding me, too. Or maybe I am being too narcissistic. It is possible May preferred to be by herself whether I was around or not. She spent most of her time in her treehouse or running around, God knows where. May seemed perfectly content to be alone. There are not many children who are like that and even fewer adults.

One morning, I found a lone ballet slipper at the foot of the porch. In the distance, I saw May running through the front yard, which was a mass of pine cones, branches, and other spiky woodland materials. She had on one ballet slipper, and her other foot was bare. It would be a miracle if that soft little foot survived the crossing uninjured. As it was also Maggie's foot (on some level), I decided to deliver the other slipper to May.

"May," I called to her, "you've left your shoe up here."

Unfortunately, May took it into her head that we were playing some sort of absurd chasing game. She smiled at me gleefully and ran in the other direction. I chased after her as best I could, but my speed, although improved, was still seriously compromised by my injury.

"Slowpoke," she yelled.

"Come on, May," I yelled back, "I just want to give you your goddamn shoe."

"You cursed! You cursed!" she said. "I'm gonna tell!"

I continued to call her name, and she continued to run. I was about to leave the damn shoe and give up. And then, May ran right into the well.

For ten awful seconds, I was frightened that she might fall in, but luckily she got tangled in the bucket.

Out of breath and exhausted, I hobbled over to the well. May was sitting in the bucket and laughing. Another reason I don't like children is because they are reckless, and yet another reason I don't like children is because they are complete narcissists.

She smiled up at me, completely pleased with herself. "Make a wish," she said.

"No thanks," I said.

"Make a wish or I'll tell that you cursed," she insisted. "When you go to a well, you're supposed to make a wish."

I closed my eyes and tried to think of a suitable wish.

"What did you wish for?" she asked.

"If I tell you, it won't come true, now will it?"

She couldn't argue with my logic, so she permitted me to pull her out of the well. I also handed her the ballet slipper, which she put on. "That was fun," she said. She placed her small hand in mine. "Greta used to chase me, too."

"Greta was your aunt?"

"No, Greta was me, only a lot, lot older," May said.

"Do you know what happened to Greta?"

"She went out for a swim, and she never came back." She shrugged as if to say, It happens.

I nodded.

"Greta cut her wrists once, too, but Maggie bandaged them up." She shrugged again as if to say, That also happens.

I nodded.

"Greta once tied a rope around her neck, but the rope breaked."

I nodded.

"Greta bought a gun, but it turned out to be a toy. She held it to her head, and everyone laughed."

I nodded.

"Greta sat in the garage with the car running, but Old Margaret opened the garage door."

I nodded.

"Everyone thought I didn't know what Greta was doing, but I'm a kid, not a baby moron."

I nodded.

"Did you hear my joke? Not a baby moron!"

"That's a good one," I said. "Hey, May, why didn't the baby moron fall off the cliff?"

She paused, then shook her head.

"Because he was a little more on."

"Not funny." By way of changing the subject, she knocked on my cast with her other hand. "Your cast is cool. I wish I had a cast."

"Thank you."

"I know what that string means," she told me.

"What string?"

"The one around Maggie's finger. It means that you think she's pretty and nice and that you love her and that you want to kiss her on the mouth every day and that you want to marry her."

"Is that what it means?" I asked.

"Maybe not today, but someday," she said.

"Is there anything else?"

"And that you want to make a million baby morons with her!" She laughed at this joke.

"Thank you, May. That clears things up enormously for me." I kissed her on the head and promised to chase her again the next day.

※

That night, I asked Maggie about Greta and she said, "She was thirty-five. She was too beautiful and too smart and too depressed and too funny and too sad and too much everything at once. It's hard to live that way. She wore herself out. She wore us all out."

"Have you ever thought about killing yourself?" I asked her.

"Yes," she admitted. "Sometimes, but I think you already knew that about me."

"Since you met me?"

"Not nearly so much," she said.

Without meaning to, I found myself staring at her wrist.

"I know what you're thinking," she said, "and I want you to know I would never just slash my wrists. If I were to commit suicide, I would probably hang myself with a very short piece of twine."

12.

It was July, and Uncle Jacques still hadn't come for me. At first I didn't worry. I assumed he had probably stopped off in Haiti or São Paolo or gotten married a sixth time. Jacques was dependable, but often tardy.

But then two more weeks passed.

And then two more.

The second to last week of August, I received a frantic phone call from Bess. "Where have you been? Why didn't you call me all summer? I had to bribe a guy at U to get Maggie's home number."

"I broke my leg," I explained. "I couldn't call."

"Uncle Jacques is dead," she said. "You have to come home."

I laughed. "Fucking Jacques. That fucking fucking fuck. I fucking hated him." A second later, I began to weep. He was a lousy father, but the only one I had.

"He was old, N. He was seventy-seven," Bess said softly.

The same age as Old Margaret, I thought to myself. "How'd he die?" I asked.

"A stroke," she said. "It was very fast. He didn't suffer."

"I wouldn't have minded if he had suffered a little," I said. And then I wept some more. "He wasn't even our real father."

"Not to mention, you had been pretending he was dead for years," Bess reminded me.

"There's that, too." I blew my nose on my sleeve. "You were lucky because you weren't actually related to the bastard," I told her.

"What do you mean?" Bess asked.

"In the *biological sense*."

"Oh, come off it, N.," Bess yelled. "You know I hate it when you play that game."

In point of fact, Jane, Bess *is* your aunt in the biological sense. Although I like to joke about this from time to time, she is, and has always been, my sister. If I lied to you before, it's because I did not want you to feel that Bess's weight problem was your destiny as well. When you have children of your own, you will understand the importance of story-telling. A child will believe what you tell her about herself, so you must be careful in this respect. When

I was a child, my uncle Jacques told me I was "sexually unethical" like my mother and "a pathological
liar" like my father, and in varying degrees, I have
worn these titles my entire life.

The night before I left for Jacques's funeral, I couldn't
sleep, so I went down to the kitchen. I found Marge
sitting alone at the table, drinking a homemade
margarita. She was crying out of her one good eye
and made no attempt to conceal her tears.

I asked her what was wrong.

"I'm a little unhappy today," she said, "but I'm
sure it will pass."

"I'm sorry," I said.

"Don't be sorry. Everybody's unhappy. It's just a
matter of extent."

"My uncle's dead," I told her.

She poured me a margarita. "Drink," she
ordered.

I did.

"I don't like men mush," she said. She was only
a little drunk at this point.

"What's 'men mush'?" I asked her.

"You are very handsome, but I don't like men mush," she repeated.

Two margaritas later, she started to get a bit noisy.

"I want to travel!" she yelled. "I want to see the world!"

I couldn't help thinking she would only ever see half the world on account of having one eye.

Two more margaritas later, she was depressed again.

"I hate Margaret Towne," she said. "I wish I could leave. Everyone here's so boring, and I'm so boring." She laughed. "There's no chance you'd like to have sex with me, is there? Maggie wouldn't have to know."

I shook my head.

"I prefer women anyway. Just kiss me then, okay?"

I kissed her gingerly, my lips barely grazing her cheek.

"It doesn't do any good to be disgusted by me. Remember that time you took Maggie to your friend Paul's house, and she drank too much and she told that stupid story about the monkeys in Africa, and you were embarrassed by her?"

I remembered.

"Well, that was me that night," she said. She had now entered a belligerent phase of her drunkenness. "That was all Marge! I can come out at any time! You're lucky you're leaving now while you still can."

"On that note, good night, Marge," I said. I stood, but Marge pushed me back into the chair.

"It'll be all Marge all the time, just you wait and see, big boy. It'll be a fat ass and fat-ass kids and foul smells and bad hair and bitterness and screaming and yelling and a dirty bathroom sink."

I pushed Marge off me. "You're drunk," I told her. "You're drunk and you're disgusting." I limped up the stairs as fast as I could.

"I'M WHAT YOU HAVE TO LOOK FORWARD TO, AND DON'T YOU FORGET IT!" Marge yelled after me. She opened her blouse and flashed her fat, fleshy, wrinkly tits. They stared at me accusingly.

Maggie flipped on the lights as I opened the bedroom door. "Are you all right?" she asked. No matter how late it was, she always pretended to be awake when I returned.

"Marge has really enormous tits," I told her.

Maggie laughed. "You seem scared."

"Well, they were just really, really big and they seemed to come at me from every direction. I just wasn't expecting it." I cupped one of Maggie's regular-sized breasts in my hand. I held it up to my eye and wondered, Do you have *that* inside of you?

It was staggering to think that all these Margarets could really be one woman. How could one woman want so many different things? Was every woman like this? So schizophrenic and scatter-brained? In any case, I was glad to be leaving for Jacques's funeral.

That night, I dreamed of L___, my girlfriend before Maggie. I dreamed of her normal-sized tits and her white-blond hair that smelled like grass and her light blue eyes and her dead, empty voice and her even, blank expression. Sweet, stupid, simple L___. I woke up with the world's most enormous hard-on. If it hadn't been four in the morning, I probably would have called her right then.

13.

The next day, I flew back to Boston for the funeral. I had been fitted with a more manageable walking cast the week before, so flying was no longer an issue. It was a little sad watching the doctor saw through the signature-covered plaster. I have never been very sentimental though, and keeping a soiled cast seemed a disgusting and pointless gesture. (In retrospect, I rather wish I had kept it.)

Despite any lingering doubts I might have had about her driving, Maggie was my chauffeur to the airport.

"Will I see you again?" Maggie asked me at the gate.

"Of course you'll see me again."

"If you don't want to come back, you don't have to," she said. "Obviously, you've been here longer than you planned already. I know this can't go on forever, and this funeral might be a natural end point for us."

"I'm coming back, Maggie. I'm coming back."

"Oh, I almost believed you! I believed you until you said it the second time." She laughed. "If you never come back, I won't hate you, you know."

"Thank you," I said.

"Not much at least," she added.

"You could come with me," I said.

She smiled for a second and then shook her head. "That was kind of you to say, whether you meant it or not. And whether you meant it or not, it doesn't really matter."

"I didn't really mean it," I joked.

"That was funny," she said in a tone that indicated it was anything but.

My plane began boarding. Instead of kissing me, she shook my hand. "I love you," she said, "and no matter what happens, you can take that on your travels."

I am sure that Jacques's funeral will go down as one of the worst funerals in the history of funerals.

One, everyone was in a bad humor, because it was muggy, hot, and humid as only Boston in August can be. And two, no one wanted to be there because no one really cared that Jacques was dead. While intermittently charming, he really *was* an asshole.

The funeral truly began when Jacques's first wife and fifth (last) wife almost came to blows over who should be allowed to sit in the center front pew. Each contended that she was the "real" wife. In the end, neither got the chair. It was given to Jacques's only biological child, the anorexic, chain-smoking Amelie, who really couldn't have cared less where she sat.

The funeral truly ended when Jacques's third wife had a minor stroke and had to be taken away in an ambulance.

Of the six pallbearers, I, a professional grad student with a still-compromised leg, was by far the strongest. The other five pallbearers were my sister, Bess, who is five feet tall, three old war buddies of Jacques's (the first had just had hip replacement surgery, the second had a trick knee, and the third had a prosthetic arm); and, of course, the anorexic, chain-smoking Amelie. Under normal circumstances, Bess would have been the strongest, but the night before Jacques's funeral, she had been savagely attacked by spiders while she slept. Her face was so swollen she could barely open her eyes.

The six of us had to carry the coffin up a hill. It

had rained the night before (*"Après moi, le déluge,"* Bess whispered hoarsely to me), and the path was basically a mudslide. At one point, we dropped Jacques's coffin, and it slid all the way back down to the bottom of the hill. I was tempted to tell everyone to just leave him there. Huffing and puffing, Amelie sat on her father's coffin and proceeded to smoke two cigarettes. No one particularly objected. "Fucking Jacques," Amelie cursed with the same Belgian accent as her father, "that fucking, fucking fuck."

It was only after the funeral was over that I noticed L___ was there. When I first met Margaret, I had just broken up with L___. It was an awful time: there are only so many ways you can tell someone it's over. I hadn't seen L___ in almost a year.

Since that time, she had lost weight and she wore her white-blond hair in a ponytail, a style that was becoming to her. Her eyes were light blue, clear and empty, against her dark dress. L___'s eyes were so light, they made her seem in a perpetual state of surprise.

She waved at me.

"I would kiss you, but I'm sweating like a pig," I told her.

She kissed me on the cheek. "I'm sorry about Jacques, darling."

I shrugged.

"What happened to your leg?"

"It's a long story," I said.

"Well, I can see that."

"You didn't have to come, L___. I was actually related to the asshole and I almost didn't come."

"I always liked Jacques," she said. "He was nice to me. Whenever we saw him, he always hugged me."

"He was just trying to feel your breasts."

"Don't be vulgar. I don't like you when you're that way." L___ shook her head. "Are you still with that same girl?"

I hesitated to answer.

"Is that a difficult question?" She raised one perfectly plucked eyebrow.

"More than you know."

"You know what I think? I think you just make things difficult for yourself," she said.

"You're probably right."

"If you're still with that same girl, why didn't *she* come to the funeral?" she asked.

I shook my head. "Let's not talk about her."

"What was her name again?" she asked.

I could tell she knew perfectly well what Maggie's name was, but for whatever reason, she wanted to act as if she didn't. "Her name is Margaret."

"Oh, of course, Margaret!" L___ laughed. "Margaret Towne, right?"

I nodded.

"Margaret's a sort of common name, isn't it?"

"Is it?"

"Well, not common like low. I just meant, a lot of people have it."

Oh L___, you were always so transparent! Your transparency was your entire charm, I suppose. God forgive me, I decided to have sex with L___ again right then.

"You look good," I said to L___.

"Do I?" Her voice was hopeful.

"You do, and what's more, I've really missed you." And in a way, I had. Sleeping with L___ was almost as good as masturbating; she asked for nothing and she took nothing; she was peaceful; she was easy.

She was easy; she was boring. I fucked her and thought of my Maggie, my sexy, messy, complicated girl. Knowing she was crazy and cursed, knowing she could one day (any day!) be Marge or Old Margaret, knowing she had little Mias and Mays inside of her, I loved her. I *loved* her. I loved her and I missed her so much. I missed her so much I almost couldn't breathe.

"Was it okay?" L___ asked me after we were done.

It's awful to say, but I had forgotten L___ was still there. I had used her and now I just wanted her to disappear. Poor, simple L___.

Jane, I am ashamed of the way I treated L___ that night. And actually, you may as well know the truth: when I first met Margaret, I was still engaged to L___. L___ had proposed to me, but it still doesn't justify my actions.

If you had known me back then, I fear you wouldn't have liked me much. You are a person of quality, I can tell, and in those days, I was not.

After I left L___'s apartment, I decided to call Maggie, even though it was the middle of the night. "There was someone before you," I began.

"Of course there was," she said.

"I mean, right before you. And a little bit during you, too. Her name was L___, and—"

She interrupted me. "I knew."

"You knew?"

"How could I not?" she asked. "It didn't matter to me. I was foolishly, stupidly, hopelessly in love with you. It was beyond reason or common sense. Christ, N., of course I knew."

She knew.

"Does it make you like me less that I knew about L___?" she asked.

"Why would it?"

"Because it means I knew and I didn't care."

I laughed. "You give me too much credit."

"But it wasn't entirely my fault, either. You played a dirty trick that day. You came into that room and you never mentioned her, not once. If you had mentioned her right off, maybe, just maybe . . . Oh, but probably not.

"I decided that day that I loved you, and for me, there was no going back from that," she said. "And I know you. You're going to say that that isn't love, not really, but I thought it was, so what possible difference can it make if it was or if it wasn't?

"You look into a man's eyes, and your whole life is there. I knew nothing about you; I just had this feeling that I had always known you and that I would always know you. I looked at you, N., and I didn't even care what I didn't know. I didn't even care that much if you didn't love me. Isn't that stupid? Aren't *I* stupid? I loved you the moment you walked into that room."

"But you wouldn't have cared if I didn't love you?" I asked.

"It would have been a tragedy. Don't mistake me. I only meant, I loved you without even knowing if you would love me back. I loved you on spec. And at first, it looked pretty bleak where we were concerned. It looked impossible, like too much had already been set into motion. I almost hated you then—for not knowing I would come along—but I never quite could."

"Thank you for not hating me," I said.

"Thank you for not hating me," she repeated. "That's just a fancy way of saying 'I love you,' isn't it? How romantic."

"I'll be back soon," I promised her.

"Oh," she began, and then she paused. I thought, for sure, she was going to ask when soon was, but instead she said, "I'll leave the porch light on for you, N. It's hard to find us in the dark."

"But I haven't said which day I'm coming back," I said.

"I'll leave it on *until* you're back," she said.

It's all decided in two or three moments, Jane. Your mother in the twin and your mother in those boots and your mother on this night. And God help me, that's love. Or something very like.

❧

The next morning was the reading of the will. If I hadn't mentioned it before, Uncle Jacques was loaded. Among other things, I inherited a town house on Boston's tony Charles Street, three old convertibles, and a sum of money large enough that I would never have to work again.

That afternoon, I bought Maggie an engagement ring, a real one. The band was platinum and looked like a piece of twine. The stone was a single pearl.

I tell you, my Jane, I liked everything to do with proposing: the buying of the ring, the getting down on one knee, the posing of the question. I did not necessarily expect I would, but I did. I liked being able to do these things for her. I liked their conventional nature after our somewhat unconventional courtship.

I liked the ritual. I felt as if I had joined some grand tradition of brave and foolish souls.

14.

Maggie put the ring on her finger and stared at it. "When does a pearl become a pearl?" she asked.

"When they sell it in a store for a thousand dollars and call it a pearl," I answered.

"I'm serious. When does it cease to be a speck of dirt, an irritant to an oyster? What is that moment?"

"I suppose when it gets that first coating of pearliness."

"But is that strictly a pearl? Isn't it too small to be called a pearl?"

"It's a pearl, M., trust me. It just needs time to make more layers. A pearl has many smaller, vestigial pearls inside it."

"I wonder if the pearl knows. I wonder if the pearl senses that it is no longer just dirt."

"I doubt the oyster cares either way," I joked.

She ignored me as I was unnecessary to her argument. "I think the pearl always knew. I think you can't be destined to be a pearl and not know it.

In a way, it was always a pearl even before it was a pearl."

"Maggie, will you marry me or not?"

She laughed kindly and then whispered in my ear, "I will, but I had to play with you a bit first. I haven't forgotten your goddamn string, you know." Maggie narrowed her eyes and then she laughed some more.

I went to find Old Margaret to tell her the good news. She was in none of her usual places. I finally located her in her bedroom: she was dead. She had died in her sleep. Presumably, it was that long-awaited second heart attack. Or maybe it was just that annoying catchall, old age. I spotted her red lipstick on the nightstand, and out of respect, I decided to give her a fresh coat.

I went to find the other Margarets. I was debating whether to tell them the good news or the bad news first.

In Mia's room, there was a note on the desk. "Won painting scholarship to art school. Met cello player with yellow dog. Don't wait up. XXXOOO, Mia."

In Marge's room, clothing was scattered everywhere. She, too, had left a note: "At long last, I have gone abroad. I shall send a postcard if I find the time. If anyone should locate my copy of *The Portable*

Gertrude Stein please forward it on. Regards, Marge. P.S. Maggie may have my crock pot. P.P.S. I'll be back before you know it." Her eye patch was hanging ominously over the mirror.

I went outside to find May. She was standing near the river.

"May," I called out.

She waved at me, and I waved back. "May," I said, "I have something to tell you."

She shook her head. Her red pigtails flew from side to side, beating her cheeks until they, too, were red. And then something strange happened. Those red pigtails flew so fast, they somehow turned into wings. And she began to rise from the ground. And before my eyes, the rest of her became a small, red bird. A robin, maybe? A cardinal? (I have never been much of a bird enthusiast.) In any case, she became a small, red bird and she flew away.

"May," I called to her, but she was already gone.

15.

As there was no reason to stay, we packed her things and drove back to Boston the next morning. I could have driven (my leg was mostly better), but she insisted on driving. She swore she wouldn't fall asleep this time; I believed her.

It was the first weekend of September, and summer was definitely over. The air was clean and cool and brittle. We had barely crossed the bridge when she pulled the car over and began to cry.

"We're getting married," she said. "I didn't really let myself feel it when you asked me. I waited to make sure you meant it. I'm used to gaps when it comes to you."

"You're the one with all the gaps," I said.

"Are you kidding?" she asked. "You tied that string around my finger without explaining your intention. You didn't call me for nearly two months after we first slept together. You never mentioned L___ at all. And as for your personal history? I've met your sister once, and I don't even know what happened to your parents. You're a complete mystery to me most of the time. I don't even know your goddamn middle name. It's just this gap between your first and last."

"It's Timothy," I said.

"Timothy," she repeated. "I never would have guessed that."

"And my parents died in a plane crash."

"I'm sorry."

"And my sister is very critical of all my girlfriends, so I don't like to bring them around much."

She nodded.

"And I didn't call you because of L____."

"I sort of knew that," she admitted.

"And I can't explain the string," I said, "so I won't even try."

She restarted the car, and we left. I suppose we must have driven past the Margarettown sign, but if we did, I can't remember. Places like to advertise when you've arrived, but the fanfare is always significantly less upon leaving. Sometimes you've left a place and you don't even know you've left it.

So we left upstate. Trees that had had fruit no longer had fruit; trees that hadn't had fruit now did.

Since that summer, I have had reason to return to this part of the country (once for a conference; once for the wedding of an ex-girlfriend), and I tell you, it never looked remotely similar.

16.

The night before my wedding, I had another "symbolic" dream. Since I'd been given that damned Dream Journal, I couldn't seem to stop having "symbolic" dreams. In any case, here is what I wrote:

> We are at the wedding. Maggie is the bride. Then I see that all the other Margarets are there, too. May is the flower girl. Old Margaret is the mother of the bride. Mia is the maid of honor, and Marge is a bridesmaid. When the minister asks, "Will you take this man?" all the present Margarets answer in chorus, "I do."

The only actual person who attended our wedding was my sister, Bess. Bess came alone; in those days, she preferred to keep her private life private, even from me. Margaret, of course, had no relatives still living.

Coming from a rather prominent Boston family, there were other people I might have invited, but I didn't want to subject Margaret to that level of scrutiny. Besides, none of these people had ever been anything more than names on Christmas cards to me. (Uncle Jacques was, thankfully, dead.) When I had been engaged to L___, her family had sent out more than five hundred engagement announcements. Mantel clocks, sterling silver picture frames, and martini shakers had poured in like manna from heaven. L___ was delighted. I do not know what became of these treasures after our engagement was dissolved. A better man would know the answer to that question.

When the subject of our wedding was discussed, Margaret said, "My interest in housewares is not nearly great enough to justify a large wedding. If you are there, I suppose that will be enough for me." She didn't want any bridesmaids either. She found them to be a morbid custom: "In medieval times," she told me, "the first bridesmaids were only in royal weddings. They all wore wedding dresses exactly like the bride, and they were meant to be decoys in case someone tried to murder her." [I still don't know if this is true. You may want to ask your aunt, Bess, who is often knowledgeable about such matters.] The only detail Margaret insisted upon was the flowers—she wanted them to be made from thin, colored papers in the style of origami.

"Why paper?" I asked her.

"Paper flowers last longer," she said, "and I'll have them forever."

"Unless there's a fire or a flood or an incident with a paper shredder."

"Besides, real flowers depress me. They smell like dying."

So, she had her paper flowers. From a distance, I couldn't tell the difference. Unfortunately, it rained that day and the counterfeit blooms grew slightly waterlogged.

"You would have been better off with the real thing," I said.

She shrugged and pulled the pulpy buds to her face. She breathed in and said, "They'll dry; you'll see."

"What is the scent of a paper blossom?" I asked her.

She breathed in again. "Nothing," she told me. "Thank God."

She tossed the paper flowers to Bess, who had spent most of the day getting good and drunk. Bess let them fall to the floor. "I suppose this means I'll never get married," Bess said. (So far, she's right.)

What else can I say about my first and last wedding? We spent the night before apart (her idea—how old-fashioned she could be!) and part of me worried which Margaret I would be marrying in the morning. Fortunately for me, the Margaret who married me that day was about my age, neither young nor old. She was a new Margaret, a Margaret who seemed to erase all others. Yet, when I looked in her eyes, I could see Marge there and Old Margaret and little May and all the other vestigial Margarets. For the first time, I even saw Greta. I had never seen her before, but I recognized her all the same. And I knew I was marrying all of them. As the minister read the vows, which always seem to me a bit like lines in a play, I knew for the first time exactly what was meant. That each of the lines (for better! for worse! in sickness! in health!) refers to all the different people you will be married to even when you undertake to marry just one.

Ah, Jane, I look back at my only wedding and I wish there had been more housewares, after all. If the presence of an industrial-sized blender and a twelve-hundred-thread-count duvet cover make it easier for a couple to stay together (or rather, more difficult for one to break apart), then I wish we had had all the housewares in the world.

When we were in bed that night, in bed for the first time as man and wife, she related this story.

"N.," she asked me, "do you know how ours was the first wedding of the day?"

"Of course." There had been two other weddings scheduled after ours at the church.

"Well, when I went back to claim my things from the dressing room, the bride from the second wedding was already in there. She was wearing the same dress as me. It was the exact same one. The same cut, the same color. Everything."

"Most wedding dresses look kind of the same, don't they? White? Poufy?"

"Yes, but I'm telling you, this was the *exact same one*. And the girl looked a bit like me, too. Only her hair was blond. Isn't that strange?"

"Yes," I said, although it didn't seem particularly strange to me after what our courtship had been like. Indeed, it seemed blissfully, blissfully ordinary. The sort of funny little thing that could happen to any bride at any time at any wedding anywhere. I imagined Maggie relating this anecdote to our grandchildren years later. Only, the story would have gotten more and more embellished by then. "The other bride could have been my twin," Maggie would say. "The other bride got nervous and fainted. The other mother of the bride asked me if I would mind walking down the aisle in place of the other bride, so I did it. I was already wearing the dress, and I tell you, the groom didn't even know the difference at first."

"Why are you smiling?" she asked. "You look like you have a secret."

"I was imagining...," I began. "I'm just..." I began again. "I'm happy," I said. "Of all the Margarets in the world, of all the Margarets who might be here today, I am glad it's you. It might just as well have been otherwise, you know."

She looked at me, puzzled. "What do you mean?" Margarettown was already a distant memory for her, I could tell.

"I sometimes think of all the things that had to happen to lead us here. You had to still be at U at the age of twenty-five. You had to have left your philosophy requirement to the second-to-last semester. You had to never attend class. You had to have a pen under your bed. You had to—"

She interrupted me. "Maybe those are just

details, though. Maybe we still would have met even if every detail had been completely different.

"Or maybe you would have met a different girl entirely and you wouldn't even know the difference," she whispered. "You'd be perfectly happy with her, maybe even happier than you would have been with me."

"I would know the difference, Maggie. I tell you, I would."

And then we had sex. I cannot report a noticeable change between premarriage and postmarriage intercourse. And for all I know, Bess is right, and you don't want to hear so much about your parents' sex lives anyway. Jane, I will tell you this, though: in Margaret Towne, I was happy for a time.

And after the wedding, you might ask yourself, which Margaret was she?

In the end, she was Maggie mostly.

She was Maggie mostly, I think.

She was Maggie, but I realized I had never really known her at all.

III. *All This Exquisite Torture*

In January, she opens a gallery in the part of town where there are so many other galleries that it is called Gallery Row. Hers will specialize in architectural remnants. She is the only dealer of such wares on Gallery Row.

A small, square, tasteful sign hangs outside her shop:

M. TOWNE

~

REMNANTS

The word *Architectural* wouldn't fit on the sign without making it look cramped, and she worried that "Remnants" alone might be unclear. It was either style or clarity and, not for the first time in her life, she chose style.

The gallery next door to hers specializes in rare books and ephemera. On the day she opens, the man who owns the gallery next door introduces himself and gives her a bottle of moderately priced champagne as a gesture of neighborliness. In return, she offers to share the bottle with him.

As he is opening the bottle, the man next door asks, "What does the 'M' stand for?"

She replies, "Margaret, but I've always hated it." (This is her standard answer.)

"They must call you Meg, then," he says. And then he repeats it, "Meg."

Until this moment, no one has ever called her Meg. She has had many other nicknames, but never Meg. She thinks about telling him one of those other names, but it suddenly seems like too much bother. And what difference does it really make anyway? If he wants to call her Meg, so be it. "Yes," she says, "Meg."

As the man pours the champagne into two paper cups, he says, "It's nice to meet you, Meg." Meg doesn't even feel like correcting him.

2.

In February, Meg's small, square, tasteful sign falls down. Ever the good neighbor, the man next door helps Meg rehang the sign.

The man next door asks, "Are you originally from this area?"

Meg replies, "No, but I went to school here."

"No kidding, so did I," he says. As it turns out, it isn't the same school, although they did, at one point, both live in the same apartment building (not at the same time). "Where were you from before that?" he asks.

"I was born in Albany," she says.

Apparently, he knows Albany very well. His grandparents lived in Albany before they moved to Florida, and he used to spend summers there. As it turns out, his grandparents' house was about a quarter of a mile away from Meg's childhood home.

"Where in town do you live now?" he asks.

"On Charles," she says. As it turns out, her

town house is next door to the town house he used to live in before he got married last April to Sam (full name Samantha).

As it further turns out, Meg moved into her own town house just last May. Her husband had inherited it from his Uncle Jack.

"I think we've spent our whole lives just missing each other," the man next door jokes.

Meg manages to laugh.

Several hours after her sign has been successfully remounted, Meg is still the tiniest bit tortured by his remark. All afternoon, it plays on an infinite loop in her head: *I think we've spent our whole lives just missing each other I think we've spent our whole lives just missing each other I think we've spent our whole lives just missing each other.* It hurts her to think of it (she does not know why), but she likes the hurt (she does not know why).

When she is back in the town house on Charles, she relates the story to her husband.

"It's obvious," the husband jokes. "If you hadn't met me, you certainly would have fallen in love with him."

Meg kisses her husband and says it isn't so.

Her husband asks, "What does he sell anyway?"

"Rare books. Ephemera."

"Ephemera," he repeats. "What exactly does that entail?"

"I'm not sure," Meg says.

The husband looks in the dictionary. "'Printed matter of passing interest,'" he reads, "'any short-lived thing.' Well, I don't imagine one exactly makes a killing in ephemera."

The next day, Meg thanks the man next door for rehanging her sign. As a testament to her gratitude, she offers to let him choose something from her gallery. "I would have picked out something for you, but I don't really know your taste. Just come in whenever you want." A second later, Meg adds, "You *and* your wife." Meg could not bring herself to say the wife's name out loud.

3.

In March, Meg has the following remnants for sale:

- 10 crystal chandeliers from the ballroom of a ship (Meg hopes a restaurant or other business will purchase the whole set; she hates the thought of separating them)
- 1 brass mirror from the commode of a 1920s brothel
- 1 mahogany banister carved with cupids, fruit, and flowers
- 1 iron balustrade from the gallery of a New Orleans hotel
- 1 sign (also in iron) from an eighteenth-century French perfumery
- More than 100 doors (most notably a set of hand-painted double doors from a church in St. Augustine, Florida; the painting on the doors depicts the story of Noah's ark)
- More than 50 windows (Meg is proud of her windows. She has always been amazed how

something that is meant to be clear can look
so different)
- 25 pear-shaped glass doorknobs from a
  Turkish bath in California (Meg can't decide
  if the doorknobs look like testicles or if,
  perhaps, all doorknobs look like testicles)
- Various hardware (drawer pulls, curtain
  rods, faucets, hinges, etc.)

The last Saturday in March, the man next door brings
his wife, Sam, to the store to choose the promised item.

"Is Meg here?" the man next door asks.

"No," Meg's shopgirl answers as she was
instructed, "but she told me you were coming."

Meg, of course, is hiding in her office, which is
contained in a loft above the main store. From this
position, Meg can watch the man next door and his
wife unobserved.

The wife is tall like Meg with dirty-blond hair
like Meg's used to be before she started dyeing it
auburn. Meg decides that some people would say
that the wife is prettier than Meg, but that the major-
ity would say that Meg is prettier than the wife. Both
women are in the same style, but Meg decides that
she (Meg) has nicer eyes and larger breasts.

The wife dutifully exclaims over Meg's inventory before finally settling on a set of ten glass drawer pulls. The pulls were from a mirrored art deco dresser that had begun to pit beyond repair. They were priced at $80 for the set. Meg will miss those drawer pulls, but she acknowledges that they were the perfect item for the wife to choose—neither too cheap nor too expensive.

"Thank Meg for us," the man next door tells the shopgirl.

"I wish I could have met her," the wife laments on her way out, "but, being in her store, I almost feel like I have."

"You would like her," the man next door says, holding the door open for his wife. "She's a lot like . . ." The door swings closed before Meg gets to hear what or whom "she's a lot like."

Lying on the floor of her office, Meg compares the man next door to her husband. The man next door is certainly not as handsome as my husband, Meg thinks. The man next door is not as intelligent as my husband, she further thinks. The man next door is poorer than my husband and fatter than my husband. The man next door has less hair than my husband.

So why is Meg spending all her time thinking about the man next door?

Meg's shopgirl comes up to get her. "Have a nice nap?" the shopgirl asks pleasantly.

The nap had been Meg's excuse. "I couldn't really get to sleep," Meg admits.

"Too bad," the shopgirl says. "You should have come down. His wife is so pretty. She looked like that woman who was married to John F. Kennedy."

"You can't mean Jackie."

"No, the blond one, the one who married the son."

"Carolyn Bessette Kennedy," Meg says.

"Yeah, her, but with darker hair."

"Some people say I look like Carolyn Bessette Kennedy actually," Meg says, although no one has ever said this before.

"Really?"

"Well, when my hair was lighter."

Head slightly cocked, the shopgirl stares at Meg. She closes one eye and then says, "Maybe, maybe. Sure, I can see that." But Meg can tell the shopgirl is just being nice. The shopgirl lowers her voice, "I know it's mean to say, but I didn't expect his wife to be so good-looking. I mean, she was *way* better-looking than him."

"Maybe he has other qualities?" Meg suggests.

"Yeah, I guess," the shopgirl says, examining her French manicure. "He seems like a sweet enough guy."

Meg wants to punch the shopgirl, but at that moment Meg's husband walks through the door.

"Now, there's a good-looking guy," the shopgirl whispers. "Your husband is so f'n hot, Meg." The shopgirl throws back her shoulders and waves flirtatiously to Meg's husband. "Hey there, handsome!" she calls out.

Indeed, most women (and some men) react to Meg's husband in this way. He isn't handsome so much as sexy. The sexy part makes people think he is more handsome than he actually is.

4.

In April, Meg and the man next door begin going to lunch together almost every day, except on the weekends. It is innocent; they have a Monday through Friday sort of friendship, those two. They usually get Chinese from the Garden of Double Happiness, which is the closest restaurant to their galleries and has a $4.50 lunch special. In addition to an entree, the lunch special includes soda and a fortune cookie.

One Friday, Meg receives two fortunes in the same cookie. The first fortune reads,

You will be wise not to seek too much from others.

The second fortune reads,

A wise man knows everything. A shrewd one, everybody.

She has received both these fortunes before. She noticed the fortunes starting to repeat themselves after about two weeks of lunches. On that same Friday, the man next door gets only one fortune:

You value honesty and have a strong work ethic.

In bed? Meg can't stop herself from wondering. The man next door looks at Meg, and she blushes.

"You look like you have a secret," he says.

He knows what I was thinking, Meg thinks. "No," she assures him, "I'm an open book."

"My wife's mother always uses that phrase," he tells her.

"Oh?"

"She always uses two phrases. The first is 'I'm an open book,' and the second is 'It is what it is.'"

"It is what it is," Meg repeats. "That's depressing somehow."

"Sam always says the same thing," the man next door tells her. "Although I don't agree with either of you. Things do tend to be as they are, after all."

"I think it's how people use the phrase that's depressing," Meg says. "No one ever says, 'I just won the lottery. It is what it is.' People say something 'is what it is' only when they wish it were the complete opposite."

The man next door's cell phone rings, and he has to rush back to the gallery.

It is what it is, Meg thinks.

5.

In May, a heavyset man tries to shoplift a medium-sized cement birdbath from Meg's store. The birdbath has two jade doves inside it and probably weighs more than 150 pounds. As Meg deals mainly in oversized items, shoplifting is not an everyday problem for her.

The man next door runs after the shoplifter and easily catches him. The shoplifter's speed, of course, was significantly compromised by having to carry the 150-pound birdbath.

Sweating and out of the breath, the shoplifter looks almost relieved to be caught. He grabs his side. "I think I'm getting a hernia," he says.

"Serves you right," the man next door says.

The shoplifter shrugs and apologizes. "I didn't think it would be so heavy."

"What the hell *were* you thinking?" Meg asks.

"I just liked those little birds. For my wife, I mean. She likes that sort of thing."

The shoplifter wheezes. Meg looks in his eyes; she suspects he is not a bad sort. Meg is fond of those little birds, too.

"How much does it cost?" the shoplifter asks. "I'll pay for it."

"A thousand dollars," Meg replies.

"Jesus Christ, you serious?"

Meg nods. It is actually priced at three thousand dollars, but Meg wanted to name a sum she thought he could afford.

"You got a payment plan?"

"Meg," the man next door says, "you should really be calling the police now."

Meg shrugs. "Not worth it," she says.

"So can I go?" the shoplifter asks.

Meg shrugs again. "Why not?"

The man next door lets go of the shoplifter, and the shoplifter shuffles quickly away.

"And don't come back!" the man next door yells.

"Thank you," Meg says to the man next door.

The man next door shrugs. "You shouldn't have let him go. It's the principle, Meg."

Meg can tell the man next door is disappointed in her. Disappointment, she notes, is the strongest emotion he has ever expressed toward her. She has to turn away from him, because his disappointment incites a strange reaction in her. For some reason, his disappointment fills her with what can only be described as joy.

And at that moment, Meg knows what she has suspected from the moment she first let the man next door name her Meg.

Meg is in love with the man next door. He saved her birdbath *and* he fixed her sign. For these services, her heart is ripe with lust and gratitude. She finds it difficult to separate one from the other.

Meg laughs because it is absurd to find herself in love with a man just because he saved her birdbath and fixed her sign.

Meg is in love with a man who is definitely no better than her husband. And yet he is newer than her husband. And in love, the newer the better.

Meg is in love! She is in love, and even though it feels a bit pointless and a bit awful, she wants to tell everyone about it. She even wants to tell her husband, as absurd as that sounds.

6.

In June, the world conspires to affirm Meg's belief that she's really and truly in love.

She sees a news report, a corny lifestyle piece, about married art dealers.

A character in a book Meg is reading has the same name as the man next door. Consequently, the book, which is very short, takes her an entire month to finish.

On a plane to a salvage conference in Santa Cruz, she is offered a small bag of pretzels. She initially declines the pretzels, but the stewardess insists she take them anyway. "For later," the stewardess says. When Meg looks at the pretzels an hour later, she notices that they are in the shape of hearts. It's a promotion by the snack distributor to link eating pretzels with a reduction in heart disease. Meg looks at the pretzels and wants to weep.

Meg suspects she is prettier and smarter than the wife, but she also knows this doesn't matter. The man met the wife first. And in love, more than most things, order counts. Still, Meg likes torturing herself with the following thought: maybe he is only married to her because he didn't meet me first?

After a while, Meg tries to condition herself to stop loving the man next door. Every time his name drifts into her brain, she pinches herself on the forearm. Although she attempts this for almost a week, the method doesn't work. She does, however, end up with a series of small and nasty bruises on her forearm. When her husband asks about the bruises, Meg says, "I have absolutely no idea how I got those."

7.

In July, Meg turns thirty-one. The man next door buys her a gift. It is an antique electric sign from a cinema in Margaret, Alabama. The antique bulbs on the front are broken and shattered, and it needs to be rewired. The sign reads, MARGARETTOWN CINEMAS. Meg approximates its age at eighty years. It has the gaudy and colorful appearance of a sign from that era. Meg loves the sign.

"I found it at a flea market and thought of you," he says. "Did you even know there was a Margaret, Alabama?"

Meg carries home the sign that night, and it causes a huge fight with her husband. Meg is always bringing home pieces that her husband deems "clutter" and she deems "art."

It's one of those Book of Genesis fights where every wrong that was ever committed from the beginning of time gets dragged out. It lasts nine hours, excluding an hour-long break for dinner.

Here are some excerpts from Meg's side:

Maybe it's stranger that you're always exactly the same. What type of person never changes? That's what's really fucking weird.

It's my GODDAMN BIRTHDAY, you asshole.

Stop complicating me! I want someone who will love me simply! You think of me too much!

And there's no goddamn way I'm spending Thanksgiving with your sister. Your sister's cooking sucks ass!

Why won't you ever share glasses with me? Do you think I'm like dirty or something? It really bothers me.

Why do you always act like I'm on the verge of collapse? Why do you see me as all fractured and broken?

I hate the way you even look at me.

For her husband, though, it comes down to only one thing. He is tired of all of her broken "crap" everywhere. He makes this point many times in many different ways using many different words. He suggests storing more of the "crap" at the gallery, but it isn't that big a deal to him, actually. Very early on (hour one, to be exact), he regrets having said anything at all and from this point forward, he tunes out everything she says.

However, Meg is determined to fight on this particular night and so she does. A good fight can be immensely satisfying. She thinks of it as her birthday present to herself.

8.

In August, Meg considers leaving her husband, but leaving a person is more difficult than you think. Money and homes and pets and hearts have to be split. The logistics of leaving seem entirely over-whelming. Meg suspects it is the hassle, more than anything, that keeps most couples together.

Meg comes to the realization that while she *wants* to have an affair, she has no particular desire to leave her husband.

Toward the end of the month, Meg's husband buys her two dozen tulips: a dozen red and a dozen white. Momentarily, Meg thinks that everything that was awful now seems fine.

9.

In September, Meg sees her husband having lunch with the woman he was engaged to before he married Meg. Her husband had not mentioned that he was going to lunch with this woman.

The woman's name is Libby. Meg watches her husband flirt with Libby for twenty minutes, but it doesn't really matter to her. Meg knows that, aside from his sister, Bess, Libby is her husband's only real friend in the world.

Meg watches Libby and wonders if her husband is sleeping with Libby. Meg decides she doesn't care either way.

Although Meg doesn't care either way, she stores this information in her head for use at a later date.

10.

In October, Meg has sex with the man next door. The sex is like any sex and feels a bit anticlimactic to her. In a way, the sex has always been beside the point.

It should be mentioned that Meg suspects that the man next door farted during the act.

The sex is consummated in the man next door's apartment. Meg is so distracted by the fart and so eager to leave by the time the sex is through that she ends up wearing two different shoes home: one is her own and the other is the wife, Sam's. The shoes are very similar, both black leather. Meg's shoe is squarer at the toe, and Sam's has a slightly higher heel.

Meg's husband notices the two different shoes as soon as Meg walks through the door.

"Hey, Maggie," he says, "did you leave the house that way today?"

"What way?" Meg asks.

"You're wearing two different shoes, sweet girl."

Her husband walks over to Meg and removes Sam's shoe for her. "See," he says.

Maggie takes the shoe from him. She realizes her error instantly and blushes. Meg's husband misinterprets her blush as embarrassment over her absentmindedness. He embraces her. "You've been working too hard," he says.

Meg stands there wearing one shoe, her own. The particular shoe she is wearing had been half of her favorite pair. She wonders how the man next door will explain Meg's shoe to his wife and if she will ever see her other shoe again.

Of everything that happened, I will regret the loss of that shoe the most, Meg thinks.

Meg stares at her one bare foot and notices a large blister on her big toe. Stupid bitch and her stupid blister-causing shoe, Meg thinks somewhat irrationally.

Meg's husband wants to have sex with her right then. And although she doesn't really feel like it, Meg agrees. She says she needs to shower first though.

II.

In November, a friend from high school, Michael, calls Meg at home. Even after all these years, she still recognizes his voice on the phone, and when Michael calls her "Mia," she is instantly seventeen again.

Michael was Meg's first love, for what such distinctions are worth. They spent a tortured two years together. He is a rabbi now and married, but he still finds time to call Meg whenever he is in town. He now goes by Rabbi Mike.

"So Mike, where do you come down on monogamy?" Meg asks the rabbi.

"Um, I'm for it?" Rabbi Mike says with a laugh.

"But is it practical?"

"Um, yes?"

"I mean, once we're married, we stop having friends of the opposite sex. You're married, and poof! Half the population is supposed to become uninteresting."

"You can still have male friends, Meg, although it's probably advisable that you don't sleep with them." If Meg is going to sleep with a male friend, Rabbi Mike thinks it ought to be him.

Meg shakes her head. "Lately, I've been feeling so tired," she says to the rabbi.

"You look tired."

"And old," she adds. "Look at me. I always knew my beauty had a clock, but I didn't think it would get so late so fast."

"I like your face better now. Ravaged."

Meg rolls her eyes. "Fuck you," Meg tells the rabbi.

"Fuck you, too," says Rabbi Mike.

"You know, Mike, I spent most of this year in love with someone, not my husband, and I thought I was going to lose my mind." As soon as she's said this, she feels better, lighter.

Rabbi Mike nods. He's used to people coming to him with these sorts of problems and is glad to be able to help his old friend.

"I was overcome. I had absolutely convinced myself that I couldn't live without him. I had no real indication that he felt anything for me, but I thought about throwing everything over for him, Mike. I really did."

Rabbi Mike nods again. In his heart, he can't

imagine the sort of man who would feel nothing for Meg.

"I had sex with him once, but he didn't love me. I knew it. He was, and is, completely in love with his wife. I don't know why I felt such a strong desire to corrupt a perfectly good man, but I did."

"Maybe that's what attracted you?"

"I tell you, Mike, it was actually one of his main attractions. How sick is that? I loved him because of his love for another woman."

"Poor you," Rabbi Mike says.

"Yet, it wasn't completely unpleasant. I was glad to know I could still love anyone like that. There's a pleasure to loving someone even when you know there's no chance of them loving you back. The pain I felt let me know I was still alive, as they say."

"Love," says Rabbi Mike, shaking his head, "it's all this exquisite torture."

"I couldn't stop myself thinking of him all the time, even though he wasn't any better than my husband. I tried to condition myself to stop thinking of him, but there was nothing I could do. I was like a junkie when it came to thinking of this man. For months, every other thought in my brain was him. And every time he mentioned his wife, I felt like he

was betraying me somehow. I felt like he was sticking
a knife in my fucking heart."

"So what happened?"

"I slept with him. And it felt totally pointless
and not worth the bother. And after a while, I stopped
thinking of him."

"Did your husband know?" Rabbi Mike asks.

"No," she says, and then changes her mind, "I
don't know actually."

"It was like that with you," Rabbi Mike says, his
eyes lowered. "I mean, it was like that *for me* when it
came to you. Even many years later, I couldn't stop
thinking of you, wondering 'what if?' It's that 'if'
that's the killer. Even when I first met Arianne, I
couldn't stop myself thinking of you, Mia. When I proposed to her, I felt like I was betraying you somehow."

Meg laughs. "We're always betraying someone.
If not the person we're with, then it's the person we
haven't yet met. And if it's the person we haven't yet
met, then we may be betraying ourselves in the
process. Does that make sense?"

Rabbi Mike shakes his head. "Not really. But what
in matters of the heart does make sense?"

"Did they teach you to say that at Rabbi School?"
Meg rolls her eyes again. Being with Mike always

turns Meg into a surly teenager. "He wasn't even good-looking, you know. He was completely ordinary. He was just a guy. Do you know something funny though? He looked exactly like you. He could have been your brother."

"That's so flattering. Let me get this straight: he wasn't good-looking and he was completely ordinary. I can't tell you how totally flattering that is to me."

"Oh, Mike, don't take it that way. I only meant, I wasn't sure how much of my love for this man wasn't about the fact that he resembled my first love."

"Your completely ordinary, not-very-good-looking first love."

"You know I love you, Rabbi Mike." She calls him Rabbi Mike every now and then, because she knows it disarms him.

The rabbi shakes his head and has to turn away from Meg. "I love you too, Mia. I'll always love you. I'll probably love you my whole damn life."

But Meg knows Rabbi Mike doesn't love her, not really. He loves a seventeen-year-old girl named Mia who no longer exists. The draw to the first love is never about the other person anyway; it is always about one's self. Rabbi Mike loves Meg because she remembers him before he was Rabbi Mike.

"Do you want my opinion?" Rabbi Mike asks just before they part.

Meg nods.

"You lied to yourself when you said you weren't in love with your husband. You just didn't want to believe you could betray him simply because you were bored."

"Maybe," Meg concedes.

"Because, Mia, there's always a man next door."

Around Thanksgiving, Meg gets what she thinks is the flu. She spends most of the long weekend in the bathroom.

Meg thinks she has the flu, but she doesn't. She is pregnant, but she doesn't know it yet and she won't figure it out for another six weeks.

12.

In December, the lease is up on the gallery, and Meg decides to let it lapse. The demand for architectural remnants was not as great as Meg had hoped it would be, and she's had enough.

She doesn't tell the man next door or her husband. She just takes down her small, tasteful, square sign and leaves.

On her way home from the gallery, Meg thinks about killing herself.

During the second semester of Meg's sophomore year at U, Meg's roommate had killed herself by jumping in front of an oncoming subway car. Meg had been very close to the roommate, and following the roommate's death, she had taken a three-year leave from school. During those three tortured years, Meg often reflected that, in suicide, the roommate had had it relatively easy. To this day (this exact day actually), Meg sometimes wonders why people get so hung up on being alive when it is so, so much easier to be dead.

Meg once tried to explain to her husband why the roommate's suicide had affected her so profoundly. "When Kat died, it somehow made suicide a more real option for me than it had ever been before," Meg said.

Her husband said he didn't understand what she meant.

"Vacations are the same way—a friend vacations in Mustique and even though you have never before thought of vacationing in Mustique, from that point forward, you see Mustique as a potential vacation destination. Your friend has gone there, so you very well could, too."

Her husband said he didn't understand what she meant.

Meg has thought a lot about it over the years and she thinks that throwing yourself in front of a train is one of the best suicide methods. It doesn't require much preparation or expense. However, it has its drawbacks, because the train could run over you the wrong way and then it might not work. You might just end up crippled or paralyzed. If you're going to kill yourself, you want to be reasonably assured of success, Meg thinks.

Meg decides that it would be much, much better

to slash her wrists. She would do it on a day when she knew for sure her husband would be out of the house. If you're going to slash your wrists, you don't want to be interrupted, Meg thinks.

Meg goes to a stationery store and buys the most expensive writing paper she can find. At home, she begins to write a letter to her husband. She gets as far as "Dear N.," when she finds she has nothing more to say.

Meg thinks, Maybe I'll just forgo the note and move right on to the wrists? She walks to the bathroom. She takes out one of her husband's razors and forces the blade out of the plastic casing. She takes the blade to her wrist. She is about to make the first cut when she finds she has to vomit.

The vomiting ruins Meg's suicidal momentum. She will kill herself some other day instead.

Today, Meg brushes her teeth, throws the blade into the trash, and decides to leave her husband.

IV. *Susurrus*

I.

In the beginning, there are two, but they do not know that there are two.

One thinks, Am I alone in here?

And the other answers, No.

One wonders if one imagined the other's answer.

And the other assures one, No.

One asks, How do you know we aren't the same? How do you know I'm not thinking you up?

And the other thinks and thinks and then admits that it is not sure.

One thinks, It seems likely that we are the same because you know my thoughts.

The other thinks, You do have a point.

One thinks, But then again, it's so dark in here, you could very well be other than me.

The other agrees.

One thinks, I hope you turn out to be other than me because then I will feel less lonely. I will always have you for company.

The other thinks, We should act as if we are two until we know for sure that we are not two. I don't think it will hurt anything.

In this way, the matter is decided.

2.

I think I can hear someone, one thinks.

It's only me, the other thinks.

Someone outside, one insists.

What's outside? the other asks.

I'm not sure. I think there might be others like us out there.

Are you sure you're not just hearing me?

No, it's someone other than you, one thinks. It isn't the way it is with you.

But—

Just listen!

One and the other listen, but whatever one was hearing before has stopped.

I hear it, the other thinks. I hear a warm rhythmic beating. A . . . a heartbeat!

That's just you again, one thinks.

No, the other insists, not us, someone else. Someone bigger and larger and stronger than us. Someone more like you than me, I think.

One listens. And one thinks, Yes, I know exactly what you mean! That's the voice I heard, too. Maybe the voice and the heartbeat belong to the same one?

Maybe, the other thinks. Hey, I've just had a thought!

I know, one thinks, I know what you think before you think it. You were wondering if it is possible that we are living inside that same one. I felt it, too. Now that I think about it, that same one has been around us for as long as I can remember.

Is that odd? the other asks.

How can it be odd when it has never been any other way? one replies.

3.

One and the other pass several weeks. During this time, one's hearing improves a great deal.

The other sleeps more than one, and it is while the other is asleep that one hears a strange sound indeed. It is a deep voice, broken and melancholy. And yet, one finds the voice very pleasant. The voice says,

> So it ain't no use in calling out my name, gal
> Like you never done before
> And it ain't no use in calling out my name, gal
> I can't hear you anymore

One kicks the other for one now has the use of feet. Wake up! Wake up!

What? the other asks.

Listen.

> I'm a-thinkin' and a-wond'rin', walkin' down the road
> I once loved a woman, a child I am told
> I give her my heart, but she wanted my soul
> But don't think twice, it's all right

What is it?

It's ... these pleasing sounds with words and something else, too. Oh, I don't know how to describe it. One gropes for a word that expresses what it is and all at once, it comes to one: it's music!

I can't hear it, the other admits.

What do you mean?

I can't hear as well as you. My ears aren't so good yet.

One feels sorrow that the other can't hear the music. And then, one has a brilliant idea: I'll hum it for you.

Can you do that?

I don't know, but I'll try.

One tries to hum the song. Oh dear, one thinks, it isn't at all the same when I do it.

I like it, the other thinks. Please don't stop.

And so one does one's best impression of Bob Dylan, although one doesn't know who Bob Dylan is yet. One finds it difficult to impersonate Bob Dylan without a guitar or a harmonica or words or very developed vocal cords.

In the outside world, Margaret turns off her record player. She thinks she might be hearing the first sounds her babies have ever made. She wonders if this is even possible at this stage and decides to check her child development book later.

"Hello, babies," Margaret whispers.

One stops humming. Hey, I think it's talking to us.

What's it saying? the other asks.

Shush, and I'll tell you. Okay, it says it is our mother. And it also says that one of us is called Jane and the other of us is called Ian.

Which do you want to be? the other asks.

Ian.

For some reason, I think you are probably Jane, the other thinks.

Oh all right then, have it your way. I will be Jane, and you will be Ian. Unless at a later point, we discover that I am really Ian, and you are really Jane.

Naturally, the other agrees.

From that day forward, one is called Jane, and the other is called Ian.

4.

We are called by two different words, so we must be two, Jane thinks.

We have been acting under that principle for some time, Ian responds.

But what accounts for the difference? Jane wonders. What is the difference between a Jane and an Ian?

I'm not sure, Ian thinks. Perhaps they just call us by two different words to distinguish us, but in reality there is no difference at all.

I have noticed that I am larger than you, Jane thinks. I have also noticed that I seem to absorb more sustenance than you. Maybe, to be a Jane means to be larger and absorb more sustenance?

Do you think the mother knows what goes on in here? Ian asks.

I think the mother suspects, but there's no way it could know for sure, Jane replies.

Wouldn't it be strange to have a Jane and an Ian inside you and to not know them at all?

It would be, Jane agrees. But maybe not. Maybe the mother has always had us inside, so it's perfectly natural.

Do you think we will have Janes and Ians inside of us some day?

I don't know.

Do you think the mother hears everything we think the same way I hear everything you think?

I don't know.

Do you think we will be in here forever?

I don't know.

Do you think—

Ian, I don't know!

There is so much to know, Jane. How can we possibly know all of it?

I think it is best to focus on one question at a time, Jane decides.

Do you think we will be in here forever? Ian asks.

Jane thinks and thinks and thinks some more. I still don't know, Jane admits.

I am glad you are here, Ian thinks. I can't imagine being here alone.

5.

Ian, you really aren't growing as fast as me at all!

I know, Ian admits, but in a way, it's a good thing. There isn't much room in here and if I were as big as you, it might get very cramped.

You do have a point, Jane thinks. Still, shouldn't you have lungs by now? *I* have lungs.

What are lungs, Jane?

These funny bags inside of you. I think they help you if you have to go *out there*.

What makes you think we'll ever have to go *out there*? No one said anything about going *out there*!

If, Ian, *if*.

Besides, I do have lungs. They're just smaller than yours. And who needs such things anyhow?

And thumbs? Shouldn't you have more in the way of thumbs by now?

I have thumbs, Ian protests. For your information, I have had thumbs for some time!

Don't be sore, Ian. I was just concerned.

And, Miss Full-of-Herself-with-Her-Big-Thumbs-and-Lungs, I have something else that you don't have!

Yeah, what?

I have an extra thumb between my legs.

Weird, Jane thinks.

And so she discovers the difference between an Ian and a Jane. But to her, it is little more than a technicality.

6.

Ian thinks, I love you, Jane. I love you more than any other in the world.

I'm the only one you know.

That's not true. There's the mother and the music and probably even more others besides.

Yes, but you don't know them, not really. If you knew them as well as you knew me, you might love them, too.

But isn't it wonderful that of all the others in the world, you and I find ourselves here together?

It is wonderful, Jane agrees.

Please don't ever leave me, Ian pleads.

Where would I go?

Out there, Ian thinks.

I could never go anywhere without you, Ian. Let's stop thinking of such things. Let's kick the walls instead.

Ian agrees.

"They're kicking," Margaret says. "Hey, get over here and feel this!"

Ian grows tired very quickly and has to stop kicking. And Jane doesn't feel like kicking alone.

7.

It is August, and Margaret is hotter than she can ever remember being. She feels as hot as the sun.

Actually, she feels like the sun. No, she feels like a planet. No, the universe. Margaret is a universe unto herself. She is a life-sustaining force. She is God. And not any old Greek or Roman god, not one minor goddess in a collective of other gods. She is THE GOD.

And in her whole life, God can never remember feeling so whole, so one.

And God loves to be naked because clothes are hot and needlessly binding and seem like a ridiculous charade to her.

Indeed, everything and everyone that came before seems that way. And nothing that came before meant a goddamn thing.

8.

I don't mean to be rude, but it's getting rather cramped in here, Jane thinks. It is entirely possible that we may have to go elsewhere very soon.

What do you think it will be like out there? Ian asks.

Jane is upbeat: Well, I know there is music, and our mother seems pleasant enough, and you'll be there, of course. I'm rather looking forward to it, actually.

Aren't you at all frightened?

Why should I be?

Well, really, Jane, anything could be out there, anything at all. And what if they're all as big as our mother? In here, it's warm, and there's plenty to eat and good conversation and—

Jane laughs. Ian, it's going to be splendid, I promise.

At best, Ian is cautiously optimistic.

Meanwhile, the world whispers, "It is soon; it is soon; it is soon; soon, soon, soon, soon, soon." And everyone can hear the world's refrain, that inevitable susurrus, even Ian.

9.

The time has come, but Ian is still not ready.

I am glad I met you, Ian thinks. Even if I had met all the others, there was never anyone for me but you.

Why do you speak as if we will be parted? Jane asks.

I am so glad we've spent this time together, Ian replies.

Stop with the nonsense! You're scaring me!

The thing is, Jane, I didn't want to mention this before. I tried not to even think it for fear you would know. But you see, my lungs never really grew in the right way.

So?

Well, it seems that a person *out there* might need such things, after all. And I'm still very, very small, if you haven't noticed.

So you're small! Maybe it's just taking you extra time to grow? Jane feels desperate.

I think my time is about up, Jane.

Jane begins to kick the wall as hard as she can. "HE CAN'T BREATHE!" she screams, but no one hears her or would understand her, if they could.

Ian, I don't want to go where you can't follow.

I'll try, Jane, but I don't think I'm going to make it.

DON'T THINK THAT!

I've thought a lot about it.

HOW? WHEN? I KNOW EVERYTHING YOU THINK.

In the part of me that not even you could know. I've thought a lot about it, and I think that most others come into this world alone and with no one, Jane. We have been very lucky in our twindom, you see. I know we have never known anything else, so it is difficult to see that it might just as well have been otherwise. We might have had to meet *out there* like everyone else. And *out there*, we might have missed each other altogether. We might have met others who distracted us. We might have been too early or too late or—

Ian, Ian, Ian, Ian. Oh Ian!

And these days have been very sweet, haven't they, Jane? I think this is what they call happiness.

Jane has never heard that word before, but somehow she knows that he is right.

And in Margaret Towne, Jane was happy for a time.

v. *A Man on Paper*

I.

When Margaret and I were first married, everyone always wanted to know how we met. There were two stories: the short story she fashioned for cocktail parties and the long story, the real one.

I have already told you the long story, Jane. Here is your mother's short version. She would say, with a knowing smile on her face, "It's such a cliché really. He was *my teacher*, if you can believe it. He was *my teacher* in a required philosophy course I needed before I could graduate. It was either sleep with him or fail. Sleeping with him seemed the better option at the time." Margaret's version was usually met with warm laughter. On some level though, I always found this story slightly insulting.

People seem to think it matters how a couple meets, but I have always been much more interested in how one parts. In general, I think endings tend to be more informative than beginnings. And yet, people love those meeting stories, even though they are all the same. It's always "a friend introduced us" or "we hated each other at first" or "I was in love with him from the moment I saw him" or "we were just friends."

I think that's why people love these stories actually. People love to hear them, because the stories are all the same—the stories remind us of ourselves.

Maybe ending stories are all the same, too. "I fell in love with someone else" or "I woke up one morning and I didn't love him anymore" or "She died" or "He died" or any combination therein.

2.

The day after our wedding, we flew to Bali for our honeymoon.

On the plane, I had another one of my pretentious and portentous dreams. Here is what I wrote in that recurring Dream Journal:

> Maggie is made of wood and you can open her in the middle. She is a Russian nesting doll. (I think they call them Matryoshka dolls, too.) Inside Maggie are many other smaller Maggie dolls. I recognize some of them from Margarettown, but there are many more Maggies, too. Hundreds and hundreds of Maggies. I open each layer of the doll, but I can never seem to reach the core.

[Jane, does the act of owning a Dream Journal somehow cause "significant" dreams?]

The first morning of our honeymoon, I awoke to find a middle-aged woman lying in the bed beside me.

"WHO THE FUCK ARE YOU?" I yelled.

The middle-aged woman rolled over slowly. She opened her greasy lids and looked at me. "I'm tired," the middle-aged woman said, "but as long as you're up, would you get me some coffee?"

I was tired *and* jetlagged, so you can see why I might not have recognized Marge at first.

I smiled tightly at Marge and went to get the coffee. By the time I got back Marge was Maggie again, but the damage was done: I knew she could slip into Marge at any time.

"Was something wrong before?" Maggie asked me.

I shook my head.

It certainly wasn't the last time she would be Marge. Throughout our married life, she was often Marge in the mornings.

3.

Real intimacy is getting to see things about another person that no one else gets to see. Sometimes, you don't even want to see these things. Real intimacy is the mustache that she shaves and the real size of her bra and the boil on her ass and the color that she dyes her hair.

In our sixth month of marriage, I found out that Maggie wasn't a "real" redhead. One morning, I found her in the bathroom with an apple-red paste in her hair. On the bathroom counter was an empty box of Medium Rich Auburn, Shade #180.

"I thought you were a natural redhead," I said.

"Well, I'm not."

"Oh," I said. "That dye looks really red. Are you sure that's the right color?"

"It washes out lighter," she said.

"Are you sure?"

"I've done this before, you know," she said. "I'll be out in another twenty-two minutes, okay?" She gently pushed me out the door.

I never mentioned the hair dye again.

I suppose I should have suspected before then. Less than two percent of the population are "natural" redheads. More damning, her pubic hair had always been a blondish brown. All I can say is that sometimes we see the signs and we choose to ignore them.

For the rest of our marriage, though, I blocked this scene from my memory.

4.

Not long after our second anniversary, Margaret came in carrying a large rectangular parcel, wrapped in plastic.

"What's that?" I asked her.

"It's a sign," she said. She set the parcel on the dining room table and unwrapped it. It was indeed a sign—a rather large, old-fashioned one with the words formed entirely of thick glass lightbulbs. Many of the bulbs were cracked or broken off entirely. The sign said, "MARGARETTOWN CINEMAS." The "M" and the "N" in MARGARETTOWN were entirely gone.

"Do you like it?" she asked.

"What are you going to do with it?"

She shrugged. "Don't know yet, but it seemed too perfect to throw out. A remnants guy I know in Georgia sent it to me. It came from an old movie house that was being torn down in Margaret, Alabama." She smiled a strange, secret smile. "Did you even know there was a Margaret, Alabama?"

"No."

"I'm going to have my electrician look at it. Maybe he can get it in working order?"

"And then what?" I asked.

"And then it will work." ·

"Christ, Margaret, don't we have enough crap that doesn't work already?"

"Is that what you think?"

"Yes." I paused. "No—"

She interrupted me. "And you can't see at all why this sign might be different to me?"

I sighed. "It's very clever that it says your name, but it's dirty and old and broken. You know you'll set it somewhere and forget about it, and it will just get dirtier and older and brokener."

"Fuck you," she said in a perfectly clear and pleasant voice. With that, she picked up her old, broken sign and left.

5.

Margaret left me months before she actually left me. The packed suitcase? The key on the counter? Only afterthoughts.

The night I knew for sure she was cheating on me, she came home wearing two different shoes. A high-heeled loafer that was hers and a pump belonging to another woman, presumably the paramour of Margaret's lover. She looked guilty and sexy, standing there in those mismatched shoes. I had never desired her more.

I suspected Margaret was planning to cheat on me months before she actually did. There was a certain smile she would get, a smile that I knew was not for me. There was a certain look in her eyes, secret and distant. Once, I know she saw me eating with L___ in a restaurant. I saw her, but she didn't know I had seen her. She saw me, but she pretended not to see me. I had not told her I had planned to eat with L___ that day, and she never mentioned that she had seen me either. Only a woman who no longer loves you doesn't care about secret lunches with ex-fiancées.

I saw Margaret's lover only once. He was at a cocktail party Margaret had thrown to promote her gallery. I knew him right away. It was not his behavior but hers toward him that was the giveaway: a certain laugh (too long, too loud), a certain attention that she paid him, a certain posture, a certain focus. You see, I knew very well what Margaret looked like when she was in love.

The lover was older than me and balder than me. I will admit that he was slightly taller than me. The day after I saw him, I called L___, and we agreed to meet at her apartment.

The question is not why I felt the need to have sex with L___ after seeing Margaret's lover (that should be evident); the real question is why L___ let me.

"Why do you let me treat you this way?" I asked her after we were done.

"You've been awful to me, I know," she said, "and I know perfectly well I should send you away and never see you again or talk to you again. I know I don't have any . . . What's the word? Self-respect?"

"Dignity?" I suggested.

She laughed. "Well, I wasn't planning to go that

far, but sure, dignity." She shook her head. "*Dignity*. Jesus. At least now I know how you think of me."

"Oh, L___!" I protested.

"I love you, I guess, and it doesn't matter so much that you don't love me. I'll take what I can get." She laughed knowingly. "You know, I wish I had never fallen in love with you, but I did. Falling in love with you was the easiest thing in the world. For me, it was like tripping over a log. Once I had tripped, it was sort of hard to un-trip."

"Margaret is in love with someone else."

"I know," L___ said. "Why else would you be here?"

"And you don't care?"

"Of course I care, but there's nothing I can do about it." L___ got out of bed and started brushing her long, white-blond hair. "I could call her, if you want," L___ said. "I could call her and make a scene." She pulled her hair into a ponytail.

"I've always loved your hair that way," I said.

"If I called her and made a scene, maybe she would forbid you to ever see me again, even as friends."

"How would that help me?" I asked.

"Darling, it wouldn't be for you," she said. "It would be for me." She looked at me with those sad, blank, blue eyes. "I wish you had a brother, so I could love him. Even a widowed father or a cousin. Someone like you whom I could love instead of you. But I can't love you anymore. I just can't. And I don't want to love anyone else either."

"Oh L____, stop being so dramatic. No doubt, you are doomed to love again."

"Doomed? That's an awful thing to say."

"Doomed, blessed. It's only your perspective."

"You wouldn't say that if Margaret left you," she said bitterly.

"Then you must remember to say it to me."

Why did I have sex with L____ anyway? Because I wanted to, of course. And because I felt entitled to, having slept with L____ so many times before. It's like driving past your childhood home—the temptation to stop and see where the new people have put the sofa is great indeed.

But mainly, it had nothing to do with L____. I think I just wanted to give Margaret a reason to leave me. And I wanted to know, if given a reason, would she use it?

She did, Jane. She left me, and I tell you she looked almost relieved.

A week after our tryst, L___ called Margaret as I suspected she might.

"I slept with your husband," L___ said.

Margaret laughed. "Well," she said, "he was almost your husband, too. You'd slept with him before, I assume. So really, all we're talking about is chronology." Margaret handed me the phone. "It's for you," she said.

I took the phone. "Hello," I said, but L___ had already hung up. "She's gone." I could have been referring to either of them.

The next day, I found Margaret in our living room with a mismatched set of five suitcases. Because I had been picturing this moment for so long, it felt like déjà vu.

"What will you do now?" I asked her.

"I'll go back to Margaret Towne, of course," she said.

"L___ means nothing to me—"

She interrupted, "That's an awful thing to say."

"I slept with her to get back at you."

She laughed. "And obviously, that's made things so much better."

"How could you love him? He's older than me. He's *fatter* than me."

"It was the *than me* part that made the difference."

"He's married. He doesn't love you."

"I know." She shrugged. "I've always had a gift for falling in love with unsuitable men." She handed me a waterlogged and wrinkled piece of light pink paper. "The note explains it all. I've always said the things I really wanted to say in writing."

I took the paper; it was blank. "It's blank."

She looked at the sheet of paper. "Oh, I guess the pen ran out. I didn't notice; I wrote this in the dark. If you hold it up to the light, maybe you can see the indentations in the paper."

"We could have found you another pen, you know."

"Not like this one. It was *the pen*, the one that was under my bed," she explained.

"You kept that pen?"

"I'm sentimental. The paper's from my wedding bouquet, too. You remember?"

"I do. Very appropriate," I said.

"I thought it might be over the top, actually. I ran the rest of the flowers through a paper shredder."

"Proving my point: paper flowers don't last any longer than regular ones."

"Proving *my* point: marriages based on twine fall apart just as easily as marriages based on actual jewelry," she joked.

"You'll never forgive me for that," I said.

"Nope."

"I wasn't asking you to marry me that morning, you know. I was reminding myself that in the near future, I might want to consider asking you to marry me."

"Romantic," she said. "We should have sent our engagement announcements on Post-its."

"The parents of Margaret Towne may or may not be pleased to announce her engagement to—"

"Come here, you," she said.

"Will we be friends?" I offered. It wasn't any good, but it was the best I could do.

"I'll send you my address when I've settled somewhere," she promised. She lied, Jane; I tell you, she lied.

And then we had sex, and then she was gone.

Several months after she left, it occurred to me that if they hadn't all become one Margaret, I might have been left with at least one for company. By that time, I would have settled for any one of them. Even Marge.

6.

By now, you know that I am dying. By the time you read this, I will be dead. For whatever reason, people seem to like to know what a person is dying from. Personally, I don't really see what difference it makes—when one is dying, one is dying; when one is dead, one is dead. In the end, it is what it is.

In case you are curious though, I shall tell you why I am dying. As ridiculous as this may sound, I caught an Incurable, Long-incubating, Rare Brain Fever brought on by the Infamous Tahitian Citrus Virus.

About a month after your mother left, I went on an international quest to locate her. She had promised to send me her phone number but, for reasons best known only to her, never did.

Using a portion of my inheritance, I sailed the world on a ship called the SS *Eponymous*. I looked everywhere for her to no avail. [Jane—if a person wants to be lost, she will be.]

On the way to Tahiti, we were shipwrecked. I was the only survivor. All the lifeboats had holes in them caused by the manic-depressive first mate, who, unbeknownst to us, had been stamping out his cigarettes in said lifeboats. When the main boat capsized, I was lucky enough to cling to one of the extra-long twin mattresses from the cabins.

I floated for three weeks on this extra-long twin, eating only raw fish and Tahitian lemons. It was the citrus that proved fatal. If I hadn't had the Tahitian lemons, I probably would have gotten scurvy or starved to death. But because I did have the Tahitian lemons, I caught the Incurable Rare Brain Fever. As I've come to see it, it was either then or now anyway. And Jane, I am thankful it was now, because had it been then, you and I would never have been acquainted at all.

During my three weeks on the SS *Extra-long* (as I came to call it), I had a recurring and vivid dream about your mother. I don't know why, but I actually had my lousy Christmas Dream Journal with me on the boat; I couldn't seem to lose that journal. [An aside: Is there anything more boring than someone else's journal? Is there anything more boring than listening to someone else's dreams? Is a dream journal then the most boring writing form ever devised?] This is what I wrote in the Dream Journal:

Margaret is a giant. She is as big as the whole EARTH. She is a PLANET unto herself. And yet, she is more Margaret than she ever was before. She is the most Margaret I have ever seen her. I think I'm going to have sex with her, but I'm too small. I fit inside her entirely. I crawl up into her through a gap between her legs. And inside, I find a boy and a girl. The boy and girl seem familiar to me. They are both fully dressed in school uniforms. The girl asks me, "What is my name?" Before I can answer her, the dream ends.

In retrospect, I see that the dream was not about Margaret at all. It was about you, Jane.

You are away this summer at Camp Heywood. It is your first summer away from home. Your aunt Bess and I argued over this decision for a long time. I thought you should go to camp because it would be best if you didn't have to watch your dad's slow-motion decay. Bess thought you shouldn't go to camp because you would be grateful later for the extra time with me.

You and I said good-bye three weeks ago. You were beside yourself with grief. Luckily, a nine-year-old's grief doesn't last very long. Just last week, you sent me the following postcard:

Dear Dad,

Camp is not as bad as I expected. The food is not as
bad as I expected either. We made bracelets out of
lanyards and rode a horse. I don't see why people
get so excited about riding horses. It is just a horse.
People sing a lot here, too. Why all the singing? At
the campfire, I had to hold hands with a girl who
has a weird rash, but other than those things, camp
is not bad at all. She said you couldn't catch the
rash, but of course she would say that, wouldn't she?
I miss you.

Love,

Jane

I missed you, too. I missed you so much I couldn't
breathe.

I go back and forth. Sometimes, I want to die
before you get back. And sometimes, I'm selfish,
and I want to see you. I've contemplated both sce-
narios: neither is ideal.

Dying is disgusting, repulsive, pointless. I am an
eat-shit-sleep factory that is failing to produce on all
fronts. Luckily, you will miss the worst parts (by
which I mean the most humiliating human parts like
bedpans and wet dreams and feverish hallucina-
tions). To you, I am only a man on paper, tidy and

black-and-white. The parts I don't write cease to exist.

In case you were curious, here are the five worst parts about death:

1. People find it perfectly acceptable to barge into your room and interrupt whatever you are reading or doing. Even before you die, you cease to be quite human, my dear.

2. Death is totally predictable and completely fucking boring. I spend my time watching soap operas. People say that soaps are not like real life, but in fact they are exactly like real life. For example, both soap characters and real people repeat the same mistakes endlessly. On the other hand, soap characters have a tendency to come back from the dead, which does not happen in real life, or at least, not very often.

3. Death is very painful. (It is pointless, boring, and in bad taste to describe one's pain to anyone else.)

4. Everyone around you ("the living") starts to seem like ghosts, and you feel dead before you are dead. Yet, you can't quite kick the habit of wanting to live. This is most annoying.

5. You spend a lot of time in bed, but there isn't any sex.

This morning I woke up feeling better, by the way. My death surely must be imminent.

7.

Margaret once said, "The best way to get to Margarettown is to *try* to get lost."

It is more difficult to get lost than you might think. The mind treacherously reverts to patterns; the mind wants to get you found. Every time you see a landmark, you will either want to turn toward it or away from it. You will either answer yes or no. And all these yeses and noes tend to average themselves out. More often than not, you end up exactly where you started from.

So I made what I thought was the exact number of wrong turns, but I could never find Margaret Towne again. And after a while, I stopped looking. I came home from Tahiti thirty pounds lighter and did my best to live without her.

I should say, I stopped actively looking. On the subway, I watched shoes. A pointy black toe and my heart stopped. On Charles Street, I was almost hit by a cab when a red ponytail caught my eye. Upon closer examination, the ponytail was a cheap, counterfeit, tomato red, the kind from a bottle.

"Darling," the owner of the ponytail called out, "don't you recognize me?"

It was L___. "Good lord, your hair!"

"Do you like it?" she asked.

"It's certainly red!"

"I'm glad you like it. I couldn't stand it if you hated it."

"What on earth made you change it?" I asked.

"Oh, I don't know. I just wanted to be different." She took my hand. "How are you?"

"I'm..." How was I anyway? "I am well."

"I'm so glad. I'm getting married." She held up her hand. It was the same ring we had bought together all those years ago.

"L___," I said, "that isn't the same ring, is it?"

"No, darling, not exactly the same one. But I've always liked diamonds of that cut with that setting. Just because we didn't work out doesn't mean my taste in jewelry changed." She laughed.

"Thank God for that. Just your taste in men."

"You would like him," she assured me. "He's a lot like you, only he's actually in love with me." She looked at me. "You don't protest. A long time ago, that might have hurt me a little."

"I'm sorry, L___."

"How is she?" L___ asked.

"She left me."

"I knew actually. I don't know why I asked."
L___ nodded slowly. "I'm sorry about that. Now
that I'm so happy, I'm sorry for any part I might
have had in that."

"It wasn't you. She wanted to leave me. You just
gave her a reason to do what she wanted to do anyway.
She should probably send you a Christmas card."

L___ laughed. "She did actually."

"What did it say?" I asked.

"It's silly, but I threw it out. I didn't even open it."

My heart began to beat very quickly. "L___,
what was the postmark on that card?"

"The postmark?" L___ squinted her large blue
eyes. "The postmark was . . . I don't remember. Why?
Is it important?"

"No, not really."

"A friend of mine saw her at a party last summer
on the Vineyard, I think. Actually, he wasn't sure
that it was her. It might have just been a woman who
looked like—"

I interrupted her. "Congratulations, L___. Tell
me where you're registered, and I'll send you a sterling silver ladle or something."

She nodded. "I thought I might run into you
today. Whenever I walk down this street, I always

think of you. I've tried to stop myself thinking of you, but I never seem to get the trick of it."

I shook my head. "Congratulations. Really."

"I should be happy that you're so sad."

"I'm not sad."

"I should be happy that you're sad, but I'm not. Can you tell me why I'm not?"

"I can't, L____. I was a bastard to you."

She hugged me. Her arms were fatter than they used to be. "I don't love you anymore," she whispered in my ear, "I really don't."

"I'm glad."

"And you *hate* my hair!"

"I *love* your hair," I lied. "It suits you perfectly." And here, for once, I told the truth.

Hours after I had gone inside, L____ was still sitting on the steps of my town house. She was crying; I am not sure why. I was considering going back out there when my sister, Bess, arrived for our weekly tradition of dinner and guilt. She had only met L____ one other time, but she immediately embraced her. Good, old Bess. Always good for a fire or flood. [Even though she is only your aunt, I feel you can depend on her, Jane—know that Bess is steadier than either of your actual parents would have been.]

Despite myself, I followed L——'s meager lead and tried to find Margaret in the Vineyard. I dialed directory assistance without much hope. But alas, there she was: Margaret Towne in Chilmark at 75 Stoneham Road #1. No one picked up when I dialed the accompanying phone number, so I decided to drive out there.

Number 75 Stoneham, an old Victorian with a wraparound porch, was the shabbiest place on the street. It had been divided into three apartments, one for each of the house's three floors.

I rang the bell. An attractive, middle-aged woman answered the door. Her thick black hair was in a bun and, though it was chilly, she was underdressed in a black unitard, multicolored sarong, and clogs like Maggie used to wear. The woman seemed to be expecting me.

"I'm looking for Margaret Towne," I said.

"Yes," she said.

"Oh, are you Margaret Towne?"

"Yes," she repeated.

"You don't look like Margaret Towne," I told her, disappointed.

"Everyone calls me Rita, and Towne is my married name." She laughed. "I'm not married anymore, but I never changed it back. I got used to being Margaret Towne, you know?"

I nodded.

"I always hated my maiden name, Ochonueve. Too many syllables."

"Rita Ochonueve. Pretty."

"Well," she said, "would you like to see the work?"

Though I didn't know what work, I nodded and followed her inside. I felt too depressed to get back in my car just yet.

Inside Rita's living room were around a hundred brightly colored cigar boxes with three-dimensional scenes and collages in them. They were like the dioramas that kids make for school reports only much more intricate and beautiful. One had a girl doll in a blue dress sitting in a seashell. Another consisted of a wedding cake topper suspended above a rickety tower of clock faces. Yet another had a papier mâché man with red paper birds flying from his heart. And another had two skeletons holding hands as they danced on a globe. There were so many little scenes, it was difficult for me to absorb them all at once. I momentarily forgot to be bereft that the 'real' Margaret had eluded me once more.

"What are these?" I asked.

"Cajitas. It means 'little boxes.'"

"They're beautiful."

"Thank you. I've been making them since I was a girl. My whole life's in these boxes. They each represent a different time for me," she said.

I pointed to the man with the birds flying from his heart. "What happened to him?"

"Ah yes, my little birdman. He left me, but I believe he lived to regret it." She smiled. "The boxes range in price from one-hundred fifty to—"

I interrupted her. "You sell these?"

"I try to, though it's not exactly easy during the off-season." She laughed and then abruptly stopped. "Isn't that why you're here?"

I paused and decided to lie. "What I meant was, how can you part with any of them? If they're each a chapter from your life."

She smiled. "Oh, you let things go. Once you're used to it, it's easier than you think."

"I'll take the birdman."

"He's three hundred fifty dollars," she said.

"Fine. Good."

She took the diorama off the shelf and began wrapping it up in newsprint. "I can't say I'll miss him, but I can't say I won't either."

I nodded.

"What if I'd said he was a thousand dollars?" she asked.

"I would have paid it."

Upon leaving 75 Stoneham, I noticed the hand-painted sign out front: RITA'S CAJITAS. As you know, Jane, it was not the first sign I had failed to see.

On the drive back, I thought of the thousands of Margaret Townes in the world besides mine: brown-haired Margaret Townes; brown-skinned Margaret Townes; brown-eyed Margaret Townes; old, young, good, and bad Margaret Townes; Margaret Towne teachers and Margaret Towne bankers and Margaret Towne lawyers and Margaret Towne housewives.

The thought was torture.

8.

During the time of her absence, I learned what it was to have faith, to be like one of those people who believe in God. Every night I would go to bed thinking *I love this woman* and every morning I would wake up thinking the same thing: *I love this woman*. To wake every morning and know you will love the same person is an act of deliberate faith. It is an act of will. To wake every morning and believe anything about yourself to be constant is what is meant by faith.

Even if she never returned to me, I knew I would love that woman. It's sad to say, but we really learn how to love during absence.

9.

Here is the most unlikely part of the whole story: she returned to me, Jane.

"You've changed," she said.

I admitted that I had.

"Your head is larger and you're taller than I remember."

I shook my larger head.

"I remembered you as the same height as me, but now I see that you aren't. Maybe I wore taller shoes in those days? I think I did. Everyone wore high shoes then."

"You're shrinking."

"Don't say that!" She laughed and closed her eyes. "Really, you aren't how I remember at all!"

"I looked for you," I said. "You were nowhere."

"Or at least, nowhere you could find me."

"Where were you?" I grabbed her head in my hands and looked in her eyes. "Where were you?"

"Does it really matter?" she asked. "I'm here now. And most certainly there'll come another day for tales of woe."

"Margaret," I began, and then a strange thing happened. I sat down, right on the stoop, and I wept.

"Don't cry," she said. "I want to introduce you to someone." Margaret gestured down the stairs to where a small slip of a girl, no more than three, sat.

"Is it May?" I asked. She looked younger than May, but then children tend to look younger the older one gets. Were there many Margaret Townes again?

"Who's May?" Margaret gave me a curious look. "This is Jane."

Indeed, the girl on the steps did not have the signature red hair of a Margaret. She was a dirty blond. "Jane?" I repeated.

Upon hearing your name, you smiled and looked up the stairs at me. Because I could not speak, I waved.

"Isn't Jane a very sensible name?" Margaret asked me.

"Most," I agreed. "It was my mother's. Did you know that?"

"I did," Margaret replied. "You'll find there is relatively little I forget about you."

"There are some things I'd rather you forgot."

"If you tell me which ones, I'll do my best to oblige you."

"If I told you which ones, you'd remember them all over again."

Margaret took my hand and led me down the stairs.

You shook my hand, Jane, very primly, and you were polite, the way one is with an uncle or a business colleague. But I looked in your eyes and I could see they were my own. Oh Jane. Did it seem to you, as it did to me, that everything in the history of the world had led to this one moment on the steps of my town house?

That day, you were in better command of the situation than I was. You introduced yourself, and I introduced myself. Then, you asked me if you should call me by my first name or if I would prefer Dad.

We never did discuss where Margaret had been or what she had done during those three years. We never did discuss why she came back either. Although I would have liked to know, I was older and wiser in those latter days. My love for her was greater than my curiosity, and for her, I was willing to live with the gap.

10.

[It should be said that the woman who came back to me was not identical to the one who had left me. Physically speaking, the new Margaret was heavier in the hips and breasts. She had a cesarean scar on her stomach, presumably caused by you. She may not have been Marge, but she was no longer Maggie either. Psychologically speaking, the changes were even more difficult to pinpoint.

In retrospect, I have a theory about Margaret's return. I think she could feel the rumblings of Marge and Old Margaret and especially Greta inside of her. I think she could feel them rumbling back up to the surface, waiting to take over.

So, I don't think it was for me that she came back. If it hadn't been for you, I doubt I would have ever seen her again. She would have stayed lost forever. She came back for you; she came back to deliver you to me, Jane.]

II.

For the better part of a decade, I had been losing one Margaret or another, but the loss of the last Margaret was, by far, the worst.

When you experience the loss of a beloved, you somehow lose more of that person than you even thought possible. I was prepared to lose my tennis doubles partner, my dinner companion, my sexy girl. But I was not prepared for the exodus of all those other, little Margarets, Margarets I had never even bothered to notice: Margaret checking the mail in just socks, Margaret at the kitchen table eating unwashed grapes, Margaret falling asleep with a book across her face, Margaret leaving her galoshes by the door, Margaret writing long letters that she could never bear to send. [Love is in these details, Jane; if it were not so, then anyone with two legs would do.]

The casualties seemed to go on and on. Just when I thought I was done losing her, I would find yet another way to lose her all over again.

When Bess and I were children, our next-door neighbors were robbed. Curious and awful children that we were, we asked the wife of the house what was stolen. She replied, "I can't yet say. I won't know what's gone until I go to look for it and find it isn't there."

This is exactly how I felt when the last Margaret died.

About six months before Margaret's death, she really began to show her age. It wasn't so much that she looked older. It was little things, things that might have been imperceptible to someone who didn't know her well: she leaned on me when she climbed the stairs; she went to bed earlier and earlier; she lost her appetite; she stopped reading; she told the same stories over and over again.

I wanted Margaret to see a doctor, maybe even a psychologist, but she wasn't interested.

"What's the point?" she asked.

The point is you're dying, I thought.

"So I'm dying? I've lived a long time if you add it all up, and I'm ready to go. There's nothing wrong with dying as long as you don't devote too much time to it."

"You don't look old yet," I said, "so maybe something can still be done?"

Margaret laughed. "I don't look old to you, maybe! When we were in the grocery store last week, the checkout girl thought you were *my son*!"

"You're making that up."

"You just don't see me the right way. Not that you ever did." Margaret laughed. "Dear God, after all these years, you must really love me."

I shook my head. "Of course, I love you, M. That's why I want you to see a doctor."

"It won't do any good, you know. I feel old. I'm older every day; it's just life is all."

Later, it occurred to me that she had read my thoughts. Only Old Margaret possessed this skill and only in her latter days.

12.

A month before she died, I found her standing in front of the bathroom mirror, my razor at her wrist. I grabbed the blade from her.

"I thought it might be easier this way," she said. "Before it got too bad."

"It's not going to get bad," I assured her.

"I'm sorry I'm like this," she apologized. "When you met me, you thought I was just some ordinary twenty-five-year-old gal."

"I never thought you were ordinary," I said.

"I'm sorry," she repeated. "I'm not exactly what you bargained for, am I?"

"Maggie, my sweet girl, don't be sorry. We never get exactly what we bargain for when it comes to these things. You do know that, of all the others in the world, there was only one for me."

"You don't know all the others in the world," she said.

"I don't need to; I just know." I replied. "Besides

which, I was easily bored, and you always keep things interesting. From day to day, I've never known who you were going to be."

"Me neither."

"Basically, you were the perfect woman for me, because you had all the benefits of monogamy and adultery at the same time."

"You give me too much credit." She laughed. "Tell Jane some nice stories about me, okay?"

I nodded.

"Make them up if you have to."

I nodded again.

"How will the story go?" she asked me.

"I don't know yet."

"Just tell me the beginning."

I thought for a moment. "I don't know."

"It can begin simply," she said. "You could even start with 'Once upon a time.' It'll be like a fairy tale that way."

"Once upon a time," I began. "Once upon a time, I was a lost man."

"Nope. Too depressing. This is for *children*, N."

"Once upon a time, I lived in Margarettown with a woman called Margaret Towne." I shrugged. "It isn't very good, I'm afraid."

"I like that," she said. "I like that very much."

I shook my head. "It isn't very good."

"I'm going to die now," she said with a smile.

And a month later, she did.

She was either eighty-seven or thirty-five, depending on how you do the math.

Her cause of death was either old age or youth, depending on how you do the math.

Of course, there is another version of this story. (There is *always* another version.) It is not significantly different from the first except in one or two minor points. The main difference comes at the beginning, when I entered the bathroom: Margaret had already cut her wrists, twelve hours before I got there, and she was lying on the floor, dead.

In this version, Margaret also wrote a note. The note said many of the same things that I had put into dialogue form for you.

This second version is the version that your aunt Bess may tell you. I strongly encourage you to ignore it. I tell you, your mother died of natural causes, Jane.

During my illness, Bess has taken care of me. We discuss you often, and these discussions leave me feeling older than I have ever felt before. From time to time, I tell her a bit about my project here, but she is of the opinion that as my time is limited, I should devote myself to only practical matters. By practical matters, I suspect she means the drawing up of wills, the cleaning out of closets, and the taking of tea. I should add that I consider my project here to be immensely practical. In my opinion, a girl should know a bit about her parents.

"Margaret was just a flesh-and-blood woman," Bess says. "A very interesting woman, yes. But in the end, she was only flesh and blood. It doesn't do any good to fill Jane's head with stories and nonsense.

"Margaret was a flesh-and-blood woman," she says, "but she wasn't so good at real life." Bess often repeats herself when she is working up to a point.

"What will you tell Jane about Margaret?"

"That her father loved her mother very much, and that her mother killed herself."

"That's a terrible story, Bess," I tell her, "and not at all appropriate for children. A young girl should not be saddled with such a story."

So, if you ask your aunt Bess, she may tell you

this dull and tragic story about a chronically depressed mother who killed herself and a father with cancer. DISREGARD THIS STORY. Your aunt Bess means well, but I tell you, it is a pack of lies. Hers is a second-hand account. She wasn't there, so she doesn't know. You should listen to your aunt in most things, but you must be prepared to ignore her in others.

And while I'm thinking of it, I do worry that life with your aunt may become dreary from time to time.

But underneath it all, underneath the wide hips, Bess is a great gal. You must remember that she and I were raised rather cheerlessly by a man who loathed children but still had rigid ideas about how to raise them.

So I apologize, Jane. For the failure of my body and for the times when Bess may be overly strict (or overly literal) with you. Know that somewhere in the universe, a rather silly man looks down—or perhaps up—at you. And this rather silly man thinks all that you do is wonderful and exactly as it should be and finds no complaint.

13.

The week before I die, I say to Bess, "I'm thinking of going back to Margarettown."

"Margaret is dead," Bess answers patiently.

"Not the woman. The place," I tell her. I lower my voice. "Margarettown. It's one word, no 'e' at the end."

"There is no Margarettown," Bess says firmly.

"Of course there is," I say. "I spent a whole summer there. All these different Margarets lived there, Bess, and they were all these different ages, but they all had red hair. You see, my Maggie wasn't just one woman; she was about six of them."

Bess laughs. "I see your meaning now. And if you cared to look, you would find I have an Elizabethtown in me. Oh yes, little brother, your ordinary sister, your everyday Bess has about ten women in her, too. I was born Elizabeth, but no one ever called me that. When I was a girl, you may remember, I was Lizzie. When I was a teenager, I was Liz.

When I went to college, I became Bee, which I've more or less been for the last twenty years so. Except when I'm feeling very bold. On those days, I'm Eliza. And then, when I'm feeling very meek, I'm Beth. I hate those days. Of course, to my brother, I've always been plain old Bess."

"But those are just names! Margaret was really many women."

"All women are many women! I'm afraid you've never known very much about women."

"Oh, come off it, Bess!"

"We're all towns, N. And the older we get, the more people move there. Some people say that people never change, but I completely disagree. People are capable of great, great change during the span of one lifetime. And women even more so than men. Maybe it's because of all the biological changes we go through—menstruation, pregnancy, menopause. Most women are at least three whole women right there," Bess says.

"I miss her," I say. "I miss her so much, it makes my brain hurt."

"Now that's just the cancer talking," she says.

"Was that"—I pause—"a joke?"

"It was," she says. "A very bad one, I'm afraid."

"You always had a lousy sense of humor," I say.

And my serious sister Bess laughs so hard she cries. She looks like a little girl when she laughs like that. I'm reminded of Bess at age six. She had this little yellow yo-yo. She loved that stupid yo-yo, loved watching it go up and down, up and down. She didn't even know any tricks or seem to have much interest in learning any either. One day I cut the yo-yo's string and retied it as a joke. She looked so sad when she figured out what I had done. She just stood there staring at the yo-yo that would not go up and down like it was supposed to. She cried for a week. She was inconsolable. Good old Bess.

"L___'s coming to see you today," Bess says.

"She wants to say good-bye."

"Oh probably," she says. "People and their goddamn good-byes."

"L___'s a good woman," I say to Bess.

"She is," Bess agrees.

"She called off her wedding, you know?"

"I do. I mean, I did," Bess says. "That was almost seven years ago, N."

"It all blends together. Why do you think she did it?"

Bess shakes her head. "I have no idea." She

busies herself across the room. "We've got to have these windows washed. Do you want a cup of tea? If you do, we don't have any milk. They ran out of two percent at the store."

Good old Bess. My fraternal twin, whom I shared a womb with, do you honestly think I don't know what's going on between you and my first fiancée? Do you honestly think I am that *far gone*? If you are in love, I wish you would tell me. I would be happy for you, Bess. I would be so fucking happy; I would be beside myself with goddamn joy. Don't you know that? Bess, are you reading this? Do you still read my journals like when we were kids?

We never say any of the important things. We go on and on about windows and the price of milk. All the rest is left to the imagination.

"Say, Bess," I ask, "do you think I could get L___ to give me a blow job? You know, for old times' sake?"

Bess pokes her head in the door and narrows her eyes at me. "No, I most certainly do not," she says.

I wink at Bess, and she frowns. "I do not," she repeats.

"Just say you love her, Bess. Just say it. I want to hear you say it."

"Why is it so important to you?"

"I want to know you are happy before I fucking die, okay? I want to die knowing you love L___. Why can't you just say you love her?"

At that moment, L___, my sweet and good L___, enters the room. "She loves me," L___ says, kissing Bess on the cheek. "She hasn't told me yet, but that doesn't mean I don't know it's true."

14.

"'She hasn't told me yet, but that doesn't mean I don't know it's true.'" I wake to the sound of your aunt reading aloud.

"Hey, that's for Jane," I say.

Bess says, "That last part made me cry. I mean, it's all a bunch of nonsense, of course, but that last part."

"Of course."

She says, "It's a love story is what it is."

"Yes."

"Because if you hadn't been such a colossal shit, L___ and I never would have met."

"That's certainly one way of looking at it," I say.

"Do you know what would make it really good?" she asks. "If you could tie it all into something historically significant. You could set it against the backdrop of a war of some kind. A woman falls in love with a man. The man doesn't love the woman back, so the woman falls in love with the man's twin sister. It could be very political, very controversial."

"It's also about me and Margaret and Jane, you know."

"Sure, you could keep that stuff, too. But definitely think about setting it against a war, just as an angle. Otherwise, it's just a story of men and women trying to make a go of it and failing. Something set against a war is significant, important."

"But there wasn't a war at the time," I remind her.

"There's always a war somewhere," she insists. "I know! It could also be set in the *aftermath* of a war, like a little village somewhere that was torn apart by a war," she suggests.

"Jesus, Bess, stop with the wars! A war has nothing to do with me and Margaret. It never happened."

"So it never happened!" she says. "Since when does that matter to you?"

15.

You may ask yourself where Margarettown was located, geographically speaking. Once, when I was still young, I thought it was somewhere between Marlboro and Newburgh in upstate New York (this is what she told me). In truth, the geographical location may be more flexible than that, the borders more malleable. Ask any good cartographer and he will tell you, places may seem permanent, but they are far less permanent than we think.

So, Jane, if you need a map to Margaret Towne, I direct you to these writings. They are an imperfect map by a poor cartographer, but they should point you in the general direction.

16.

At the end of the day (and indeed, that is where I now find myself), a man feels compelled to share what he has learned in this life. And yet, Jane, in writing it all down, I realize how little that really is. I realize that I never knew your mother at all and that I was only just barely acquainted with myself. And now, I shall never know you other than as a girl in a plaid kilt and two dirty-blond braids. (If you ever wonder where you get your hair color, it is my own, or rather my own as it was when I was a boy.)

I wish I could tell you to always follow your heart, but I think it is bad advice. You have a heart, yes, it is true, but also a brain and also a soul. I've come to believe that we love with our brains as much as our hearts. *Real love* is not just instinct, but intent. It is more than biology, more than a glint in the eye and a quickening of the pulse.

There is a certain nobility to monogamy, Jane. A certain nobility even in the attempt. To go to sleep and wake up next to the same person for the rest of your life, to stay even when you long to go—these are the real rituals of love.

If I am making love seem very gloomy indeed, that is not my intent. Love in all its forms (romantic, platonic, self, conjugal, familial, etc.) is lovely, lovely, lovely.

So here is my wish for you.

Some day, you do not know when, you will be driving down the road and some day, you do not know when, you will make a wrong turn. At the end of the road, when you're least expecting it, he (or possibly she) will be there.

And oh Jane, my lucky girl, this man will be a city to you. In him, you will find stores and restaurants and the opera and a baseball team. And there might be a prison and there might be a hospital, too. Everything you need for survival will be in this man, oh Janest of Janes.

And when you find this place, oh this wondrous place, you shall never want to live anywhere else. Park your car, Jane, and stay. For this city will be home to you. Only not like a home you've ever known. It will be the homiest of homes.

And in this city, there will be love. And in this

city, there will be sorrow. And in this city, there will
be richer and poorer and better and worse and sickness and health and everything under the sun. This
is the greatest city on earth, Jane. And to you, if
you're very lucky, it will be the only city on earth.
The place where you're born for the first time and
the place where you die and the place for everything
in between.

For the last eight years of your life, I have watched
you very carefully. By the time your mother was your
age, she had already split into two Margarets. You, my
sweet girl, are not your mother's daughter, except in
the good ways. Rest assured, you are not cursed. You
will be a happy, singular, whole person, but you will
have a city of Janes within you, too.

From year to year, you may not always be the
same Jane. This is perfectly normal. A Jane is many
Janes in a lifetime. In the last eight years, you have
already been more Janes than I can count. Embrace
your iterations; none of them last very long, and as
your aunt Bess says, most women do have many
women inside them.

I die, Jane. The world grows more gorgeous
every day.

I am only forty-six—that may seem old to you

now, but a day will come (and sooner than you think) when forty-six seems very young indeed.

I am only forty-six and it would seem tragic, but for one thing.

In you, I found infinity; in you, I was reborn.

P.S.

It isn't long now, Jane. Soon, I will return to Margarettown. When I get there, I will send you a final letter. Make that a postcard. A postcard and you will know I have arrived safely. In case there isn't enough room to sign my name (it's only a little postcard, after all), you'll know it by the "Margarettown" postmark. And in case the postcard never arrives, here is what I would have written:

> Dear Jane,
> Your mother's name was Margaret Mary Towne.
> She was born in Albany, NY, in 19__. We met in
> college and we married soon thereafter. She killed
> herself (pills and a razor to seal the deal) when you
> were six—I am not sure why—maybe she was Greta
> that day?
>
> And that said, my darling, everything else I've
> ever told you about her is strictly, strictly true.
> All my love—

You flip the card over. It's a picture of the Margarettown sign, only someone has finally painted in the "M" and the "N". It was me, Jane, in case you hadn't guessed; I've been wanting to do it for some time. The sign now reads, WELCOME TO MARGARET-TOWN, and underneath that, POPULATION 02.

VI. *Here in the City of Janes*

I.

When Jane was born, she came out crying and continued crying nonstop for the next six months. In
general, babies cry a lot, but no one had ever seen a
baby who cried quite as much as Jane.

Jane was not an adorable newborn. She was snotty,
red-eyed, red-nosed, and puffy. The nurses moved
Jane from the nursery into a private room. They
thought that Jane's sorrowful refrain was disturbing
the other babies.

Jane did not notice that she had been moved.
She was too consumed by her own grief to interpret
the random patterns of others.

Around the fifth month of Jane's life, Jane forgot why she was crying in the first place. And, to everyone's great relief, in her sixth month, she stopped
crying entirely.

Even at six months old, it seemed absurd to Jane
that she couldn't remember why she was crying. So
Jane began to laugh instead.

2.

When Jane was six years old, her mother died. By all outward appearances, Jane was unmoved by the death of her mother. She had spent the morning of her mother's wake busily rearranging the furniture in her dollhouse.

Jane had very good hearing and overheard her aunt Bess whisper to her father, "She hasn't cried once. She doesn't understand that Margaret is dead. At that age, they can't fully understand the concept of death. It's a good thing really."

Aunt Bess was wrong. Jane fully understood the concept of death and she felt truly injured that Aunt Bess considered her unmoved. Jane thought it should be perfectly clear to everyone that rearranging the furniture in her dollhouse *was* her expression of grief. She had been moving the Mother Doll (it was a nuclear family of dolls that consisted of a mother, a father, a boy, and a girl) and all the Mother Doll's possessions into the dollhouse's attic. Jane wondered why tears were considered a superior form of grief to the rearrangement of one's dollhouse.

Feeling terribly misunderstood, Jane began to cry.

"Oh listen," said Aunt Bess, "she begins to understand."

3.

When Jane was eight, she became convinced that her dead mother's spirit was contained inside the family cat, Gato. Her conviction was largely based on the fact that both Gato and Jane's mother had the same color hair.

Jane had long discussions with Gato—mainly relating to what it was like for a person who had once been a human and a mother to now be a cat. During these discussions, Gato would lick her paws and say nothing. Jane interpreted this silence as wisdom mixed with agreement.

Around the third month of Jane's belief that Gato was her mother, Jane developed a severe case of hives.

Jane was taken to the doctor, who said that she was, in fact, allergic to cats and that prolonged exposure to Gato may have activated an allergy that would have otherwise lain dormant. Unless Jane wanted to take drugs, Gato would have to be given away.

Jane pleaded with her father to spare Gato. "It's like giving away Mom!" Jane declared.

"Your mother is not in that cat," Jane's father said.

"How do you know?" Jane countered. "They have the same color hair!"

"If that's your only proof," he said, "you ought to know that your mother wasn't a natural redhead."

"You're just saying that because you want me to get rid of Gato," Jane insisted.

"Jane, I saw her dye it."

"But maybe she was just dyeing it from gray," Jane argued.

And then, her father conceded. He was tired of fighting, and it was impossible to convince an eight-year-old that her mother hadn't been a natural redhead without resorting to crude devices.

4.

When Jane was eleven, her father died, and she went to live with Aunt Bess and Aunt Bess's "friend" Libby in Phoenix, Arizona. Jane was told to call Libby "Aunt Libby" even though Libby was not, in fact, Jane's aunt. Jane further suspected that Aunt Libby might be more than Aunt Bess's "friend."

"Sure, I'll call her Aunt Libby," Jane said to Aunt Bess. "I call you Aunt Bess, and you're not my real aunt either."

"What do you mean?" Aunt Bess asked.

"In the *biological sense.*"

"What do you mean?" Aunt Bess repeated.

"Dad said you weren't my aunt in the 'biological sense.'"

Aunt Bess rolled her eyes, which was a gesture she loathed in other people but often employed herself. "Your dad said a lot of things, didn't he? I assure you, I am and have always been your aunt, by which I mean your father's sister, in the *biological sense.*" Aunt Bess shook her head.

"If it's any consolation," Jane added, "he also said you were his 'favorite sister.'"

"Oh for God's sake, I was his *only sister*." And then Aunt Bess began to cry because she really missed her little brother very much, flawed as she considered him to be. She hugged Jane with her enormous, pillowy arms. "You look a lot like him, you know," Aunt Bess said. "I was his twin (twins ran in our family), but you look more like him than I ever did."

Jane nodded.

"He was my little brother, Jane. You can't imagine what it is to lose your little brother."

"Wait!" Jane pulled free from Aunt Bess's embrace. "I thought you said you were his twin."

"I was three hours and three minutes older than him, but it always felt much longer somehow."

Jane narrowed her eyes. "If, as you claim, you really are my aunt in the *biological sense*—"

"Jane, I am!"

"*If*," Jane repeated, "why would Dad have lied about it?"

"Oh, who knows? He must have had his reasons. He was on a lot of drugs toward the end, but even before all that, your father had always approached the truth with a certain flexibility."

"Are you saying Dad was a liar?"

"Most parents are to some extent," Bess said. "From our earliest memories, we know that our parents will lie to us. They do it to protect us or maybe out of some misguided sense of kindness."

"So most parents are just"—Jane paused—"kind liars?"

Bess sighed. "I won't ever lie to you."

"How do I know you aren't lying now?"

"I won't ever lie to you because I'm not your parent. I'm your aunt, and aunts don't lie. Go ahead, ask me anything."

Jane thought for a moment before asking, "What is the exact nature of your relationship with Aunt Libby?"

"We're...," Aunt Bess began. Although open about most subjects, she had always been slightly uncomfortable with her lesbianism; try as she might, she could not stop herself from seeing it as some sort of personal and moral failing. Consequently, Aunt Bess did not ever describe herself as a lesbian, although, in point of fact, she was. However, she did not want to start things off with a lie. "We're partners," Aunt Bess said finally.

"Do you mean lesbians?" Jane asked.

"Oh I suppose, if you must be so awfully literal, yes."

"What's wrong with being literal?" Jane asked.

"It is good to be literal, Jane, but not too literal," Aunt Bess said.

5.

When Jane was thirteen, she was asked to write an essay about a family member for school. Although Jane could have written about either of her aunts, she chose to write about her father, who, truth be told, she had already begun to forget. For the assignment, Jane was meant to interview the subject and people who knew the subject. She was wary of asking Aunt Bess about her father—Bess was liable to break down in tears—so Jane invented what she could not remember or, indeed, had never known.

MY FATHER

No one can say where my father is from because he was born on a boat. When you are born on a boat, you are really born in a body of water. On my father's birth certificate it says Place of Birth: Atlantic Ocean.

My father has a twin sister named Elizabeth. Twins run in our family—I have a twin brother named Ian. Ian does not go to our school because

Ian is a genius and does not need to go to school.

My father was on the Olympic badminton team, but he placed fourth, so he did not receive a medal. He competed for America, but he could have really chosen anyplace, being from the Atlantic Ocean as he was.

My father broke the hearts of many women before he married my mother. He is handsome (it's hard to know if this is true because it's impossible to say if your own dad is handsome or not) and funny sometimes. I think this must have been the attraction for the women, but then again it is hard for me to say.

I did not live with my dad when I was little because my mother was angry with him. My mother was angry with him because he used to be a professional spy. He makes a good spy because he is not really from anywhere and is athletic. He promised to give up the spying and then my mother took him back. But he couldn't give up the spying forever, so now he spies again. But my parents don't live together, and that's all I want to say about that.

During his lifetime, my dad had many brushes with death. (Owing to his occupation and other things of an unlucky nature.) He was almost lost at sea. Twice. Now he is a very old man with gray hair and a fake eye.

Jane received the grade of B-. Her teacher's comments were: "Jane, this essay was meant to be TRUE. Furthermore, your penmanship is below grade level."

Jane complained bitterly to her aunts about the grade, which was lower than she normally received on her compositions. "Why does it matter if it is true or not?" Jane wondered.

"I think," Aunt Bess said, "that if you are going to invent things, you ought to do so more plausibly."

"Besides which, my penmanship never bothered her before."

"I think," Aunt Libby said helpfully, "that in the future, you ought to type. When things are typed, they look more true."

The next day, Aunt Bess had a change of heart, so she decided to call the teacher and lie. "Mrs. Gerontion," she said, "I assure you, all of what Jane wrote was completely true. The only thing Jane did not mention was that her father is dead. I think, under the circumstances, exceptions must be made."

Mrs. Gerontion, who was not unfeeling, changed Jane's grade to a B+.

6.

When Jane was fifteen, she lost her virginity for the first time. She found the event completely unre- markable. The most disappointing part was that she did not bleed. And what was the point of being a virgin if she wasn't going to bleed?

After the event, the song "Don't Think Twice, It's All Right" was playing on his CD player. In Jane's opinion, the lyrics really didn't make much sense, but she still found them vaguely comforting. By the end of the chorus, Jane decided she hadn't lost her virginity at all. She would look for an opportunity to do it a second time "for real."

7.

When Jane was sixteen, she lost her virginity for the second time to a boy named Ian.

After they had finished, she said to him, "When I was a kid, I used to have an imaginary friend called Ian."

"Um, okay," Ian said.

"I used to pretend he was my twin."

"That's weird," Ian said.

As she had always been particularly fond of the name Ian, Jane couldn't help wondering if the real reason she had chosen Ian was because his name was Ian.

The second time was not markedly different from the first, so Jane decided that that would be the last time she lost her virginity.

The only person Jane told about her second "first" time was her aunt Libby, who knew all Jane's secrets. (She found it easier to discuss things with the aunt who was not related to her in the biological

262

sense.) Jane expressed to her aunt a concern that it was unethical to lose one's virginity twice. In response, Aunt Libby stroked Jane's hair and told Jane not to worry. "Darling," Aunt Libby said, "it sometimes takes two times to get a thing right."

8.

When Jane was eighteen, she went to a very good college back East.

In her first year of college, Jane did what the other girls did. She attended classes, more or less; she gained fifteen pounds, more or less; she joined clubs and appeared in group photos; she bought books and even read some of them.

In her second year of college, she fell asleep. At first, no one noticed, least of all Jane herself. But before long, Jane had been asleep for the better part of three months.

Her roommates worried over her and wondered if she had mono. Jane wished she did have mono because then she might have had an excuse. The truth was, Jane was just sleepy.

Jane didn't mean to sleep through all of her classes. She would set her alarm to ring fifteen minutes before the class began and would then press slumber right up until fifteen minutes after the class had started. At that point, she would concede defeat and turn off her alarm until it came time for the next class she wouldn't attend to begin.

On the first day of college, a speech had been given by one of the less interesting deans about how much each class cost. If you took four classes a semester, the average cost of a single hour-long class was $400. This figure tormented Jane a bit and also exhilarated her. College was the most valuable sleep she had ever had.

9.

When Jane was twenty, she wrote a short story for U's literary magazine's annual short story contest. The top prize was a pen with a clock on it and a small dorm fridge. The second prize was an ironing board. The third prize was a block of cheese. Honorable mention was a somewhat smaller block of cheese. The great debate at the office of *Sic* was whether the top prize should consist only of the pen with the clock ("It's the most literary," said *Sic*'s Cochairperson of Refreshment, "and the most classy!"). They would then shift the small dorm fridge to second prize. However, the Director of Fonts felt that, as the small dorm fridge was the prize with the greatest monetary value, it needed to remain the top prize. In the end, the Director of Fonts and the Cochairperson of Refreshment held a thumb war and a staring contest, and in this way, the matter was decided. The whole process took exactly four times as long as deciding the actual winners of the short story contest.

Jane did not win the contest or even place. Indeed, Jane's story was not very good. It was the cheapest kind of writing: a thinly veiled account of Aunt Bess's relationship with Aunt Libby, stylistically derivative of Raymond Carver. For reasons best known only to her, Jane did send the story to Aunt Bess. A week later, Jane received an eight-page letter from her aunt. The letter mostly consisted of corrections relating to grammar. Considering that Jane's story was only eleven pages, Jane considered Aunt Bess's response to be somewhat excessive. The letter began:

> Dear Jane,
> On page one, paragraph two you write, "Following sex with Aunt Lizzie, Aunt Beth always felt badly." Of course, Aunt Beth felt bad. (Although I leave this matter to you, I also wonder at the choice of the word bad, which is not very descriptive. I found myself thinking, "*How* did Aunt Beth feel bad? *Why* did Aunt Beth feel bad?" Incidentally, your own Aunt Bess NEVER felt bad after sex with Aunt Libby.)
> On page one, paragraph three you write . . .

The rest of the letter continued in a similar vein.

Aunt Bess did note that Jane's aunt Libby "loved it." This document marked the end of Jane's brilliant career as a writer of short fiction.

A week after that, Aunt Bess sent Jane a second letter and also a package. "Toward the end of his life, your father fancied himself a bit of a writer," Bess wrote, "though his writings never took a very cohesive form, I'm afraid." Inside the package was an assortment of cocktail napkins, loose-leaf papers, Post-its, postcards, note cards, notebooks, match-books, greeting cards, flyers, file folders, and even an ultrasound. On these "papers," Jane's father had written a sort of vita of Jane's mother. "I felt you should have this," Bess concluded, "as he wrote this for you and you are now old enough to make what you will of it."

Due to the collagelike nature of Jane's father's "work," Jane found it very difficult to determine the correct reading order. She did the best she could to arrange and organize it, but was constantly having to reread and start again. She also found her father's prose style to be a bit fancy for her taste. (Although it should be pointed out that Jane was going through a major Raymond Carver phase.)

After Jane had worked her way through the documents, she called her aunt Bess collect. "Is this for real?" Jane asked.

"I don't know," Bess answered. "Some of it is."

"Well, which parts?"

"I think it's more complex than that," Bess said after a moment. "I think your dad struggled to make sense of Margaret while she was alive. I think he didn't want to leave you with a sad story at your core where all your life you would be saying, 'My mother was depressed. My mother killed herself,' and think, perhaps, her actions reflected on you somehow. I think, in a sense, that this was his attempt to explain her. For you mostly, but also for himself."

Jane and Aunt Bess sighed identical sighs.

"Look," Aunt Bess continued, "I never understood exactly what he was trying to accomplish, but I know he loved you." Aunt Bess capped off this chestnut with an apologetic shrug, which Jane could not appreciate over the phone.

"So my mother wasn't eighty-seven years old when she died?" Jane asked.

"Margaret was an unusual woman in many ways, but she was just a woman, Jane."

"But what actually happened?"

"It's just a story, Jane. It's a courtship story. All

couples have them, and these stories become braided with other stories and embellished, and they take on lives of their own. And after a while, it doesn't matter if they actually happened or not. In the telling and the retelling, somehow these stories become our lives." And here Bess paused, remembering the day she met Libby. It was a chance encounter outside Jane's father's town house; Libby was about to be married to someone else. It was a chance encounter, Bess thought, feeling a chill. It could have happened or not happened, and the universe wouldn't have cared either way.

About halfway through the conversation, Aunt Libby picked up the other phone to place a different call and she began to dial.

"Libby, I am on the phone," Aunt Bess protested.

"Oh, I'm sorry. With whom?" Libby asked.

"Jane."

"Jane! Jane! Why didn't you tell me Jane was on the phone? I would have picked up earlier. How are you, honey?"

"Good," Jane replied.

"We really *loved* your short story here."

"Thanks," Jane said, "but I don't think it was very good actually."

"You can tell me. Am I meant to be Aunt Lizzie?" Aunt Libby asked conspiratorially.

"I, um—" Jane began. She always felt overwhelmed when both her aunts got on the phone at the same time.

"Libby, we were having a serious conversation here," Aunt Bess said.

"Don't stop on my account," Aunt Libby said.

Jane could hear Aunt Bess's sigh over the phone. "As I was saying—"

"Before you start," Aunt Libby interrupted. "Jane, honey, Bee and I are coming up in three weeks for Junior Parents' Weekend. I need the name of that cute B&B we stayed at last year."

"Oh Aunt Libby, you don't really want to stay at that awful place again?" Jane asked.

"I liked it. The owner was a real doll. Did we tell you that she raises Welsh Corgis?"

The discussion never returned to Jane's mother or Jane's father's writings. In a way, it was just as well. All that was ancient history anyway, and the rest of the conversation was devoted to more pressing matters like the relative merits of B&Bs versus hotels, and whether Jane was getting enough protein.

As she sorted through the ephemera later that

night, it occurred to Jane that the only concrete evidence of her mother within the packet was a cocktail napkin with a phone number and the words "In Case of Emergencies" written in cursive. She assumed the writing was her mother's, although, in point of fact, she knew only that it was not her father's. She wondered who her mother had called (if indeed she had called anyone) during emergencies. Jane dialed the number, which fortunately was local to U. (She was not able to place long-distance calls, having not paid her phone bill for several months.)

A man answered, "Temple Beth El. Rabbi Levy speaking."

Jane laughed, but did not entirely know why she was laughing. Maybe it was the thought of her mother (who as far as Jane knew, had not been Jewish) going to synagogue during emergencies?

"Hello," Rabbi Levy repeated.

Jane laughed again. She was about to hang up when the rabbi said in an unusually kind voice, "Can I help you?" And a second later, "Are you in trouble?"

"I don't think so," Jane replied. "It's just a wrong number."

"Are you sure?" the rabbi asked.

Jane laughed again. "Well, I found this number among a—" she lied here without knowing why, "dead friend's things. But the number was very old, so I assume it may have changed. And my friend wasn't Jewish."

"I do occasionally receive phone calls from non-Jews," the rabbi joked. "Maybe your friend was a personal friend of mine," he suggested. "What was the friend's name?"

"Margaret Young."

The rabbi said nothing.

"But maybe you knew her by her maiden name, which was Towne."

"Margaret Towne," the rabbi said.

"Yeah. She also used it professionally. Did you know her?" Jane asked.

"No, I can't say I did," the rabbi replied.

"I knew it was a longshot," Jane said. "Well, thanks anyway."

"No problem."

Jane was about to hang up for the second time when the rabbi asked her name.

"I'm Jane," she said.

"Jane, why don't you come to my office?"

"Why?"

"It's just"—the rabbi paused—"you sound like you need someone to talk to."

Since the synagogue was in Brookline and only fifteen minutes from Jane's dorm, she agreed to meet him the following Tuesday afternoon.

"Rabbi Levy?" Jane asked a tall man with dark hair, light eyes, and an expensive and awful sweater.

"Jane?" the rabbi asked. When the rabbi saw her, he knew instantly that she had lied about her relationship to Mia. Indeed, the resemblance was unmistakable.

Jane nodded.

"People call me Rabbi Mike, or just Mike actually."

The way he said it—Jane knew instantly that he had lied, too. He seemed nervous—his palms were moist when they shook hands—and it was clear to her that the rabbi had known her mother.

The rabbi led Jane into his office, which was covered with framed photographs, mostly of his family. Instead of sitting down, Jane studied the rabbi's pictures.

"Are these your children?" Jane asked.

The rabbi nodded.

"Is this your wife?"

The rabbi nodded again.

On the top shelf of his bookcase, Jane noticed a framed black-and-white school photo of a high school basketball team. She took the photo off the shelf to study it in greater detail. In front of the team was a sign that said ALBANY NORTH H.S. BOYS JV BASKETBALL.

"Was this your team?"

The rabbi nodded.

Jane replaced the photograph and removed the cocktail napkin from her pocket. She placed it on the rabbi's desk. "Is this your handwriting or hers?"

Rabbi Mike picked up the cocktail napkin and brushed his finger across it. "Both," he answered. "I wrote the numbers; she added the note."

"What did she mean, 'in case of emergencies'?"

"I think..." He paused. "It's hard to say, but I think she meant that she could count on me."

"Count on you for what exactly?"

"I think she would call me when she wanted someone to see her a certain way, if that makes sense."

Jane nodded.

"Did she ever mention me?" the rabbi asked.

"No," Jane replied.

The rabbi turned toward the window, away from Jane, and when he spoke, his voice was a husky, broken whisper. "I was so fucking in love with her. I still am, in a way."

Jane nodded.

"My whole life, I never could tell which things were whims and which things I should follow through with, do you know?"

Jane shook her head. "I'm not sure."

The rabbi laughed. "A sixteen-year-old gentile still dominates a forty-nine-year-old rabbi's dreams. How pathetic is that?"

"What about your wife?"

"I love her, too. Of course I love her, too."

Impulsively, Jane hugged the rabbi.

"In another life, you might have been my daughter," he said. Rabbi Mike had wondered countless times what this other life might have been like.

That afternoon, Jane left her mother's dossier with the rabbi (having actually known the woman, Jane thought he might be helpful in interpreting it) and about two weeks later, he returned the package to Jane with a note.

"Dear Jane," he wrote, "I have reviewed the enclosed 'documents' and I feel I must tell you that your father got it completely wrong. For example, at sixteen she was nothing like the Mia character (I say 'character' because that is what your father has created here) with the black nail polish. Mia never had artistic ambitions of any kind. She always wanted to be an art historian. I mention this only because your father attributes the beginnings of her depression to thwarted artistic ambition, which is entirely incorrect. As you probably know, most experts say that depression is the result of chemical imbalances in the brain..." The letter went on for another page. At the end, Rabbi Mike apologized for his outburst and encouraged Jane to call him anytime she liked. In a final postscript he wrote, "Because I loved your mother, Jane, you also have my love, and you may do what you will with it."

Jane found all of this to be a little intense. Although she rarely smoked, she asked her roommate, Cate, if she had any of that good "stuff" left. Cate did indeed, and the two girls lay on their common room floor getting nice and baked.

Despite herself and her mellow high, Jane began to reflect on her father's narrative. If her mother had committed suicide over an affair gone wrong (as her father seemed to suggest in one of his papers), was it possible that she, Jane, had never been born at all? Because in thinking about it now, Jane wasn't sure she could resolve the dates to her satisfaction. And if the dates didn't make sense, was it possible that Jane didn't really exist except as an invention of her father's?

Jane tried to express herself to Cate. "Hey, Cate, what if we don't really exist? And we're just, like, fictions?"

Cate giggled and passed Jane the joint. Jane inhaled slowly and about an hour later, Cate responded to Jane's question with another question, "But aren't we all actually fictions of each other? I mean, you exist to me only as I see you."

"See?"

"Perceive, man. It's, like, all about perception."

Jane nodded slowly and reflected on Cate's words.

"Hey, Jane?" Cate interrupted Jane's reverie.

"What?"

"You wanna get pancakes?"

The girls went in search of the pancake house, which for a variety of reasons, they could not locate. When Jane woke in the morning, she was hungry. Her hunger assured her that she was a "real" person.

10.

When Jane was twenty-one, she decided to fix the broken MARGARETTOWN CINEMAS sign. As a freshman, she had shipped the sign from Arizona to display in her dorm room. For the last three and a half years, she had intended to get the sign fixed, but for one reason or another, had never found the time. In Jane's senior year, all her winter exams had ended early in the examination period. With two weeks until the start of the new term and nothing to do, Jane decided to upgrade the project's status from ONGOING to CURRENT.

Jane touched up the paint on the sign herself, but when it came to the rewiring, she knew she would need professional help.

Cate knew a guy called King in the engineering lab. The roommate thought King could easily fix Jane's sign, so Jane lugged the sign across campus to the science building. (As a history major, Jane had never found cause to go there before.)

King was not in the lab that day (mono), but a guy called Glass was there. Glass wanted to be a chemical engineer, but he enjoyed fixing things and had some knowledge of wiring. He easily rewired Jane's sign and even told Jane where she could go in town to get thirty-six replacement bulbs that had the right antique look. When Jane offered to pay Glass, Glass declined. Instead, he offered to carry Jane's sign back to her dorm for her.

As they walked the short distance from the lab to Jane's dorm, Glass found himself wishing that the walk might somehow find a way to never end. He wished he could walk with this woman for all time.

"What's your first name anyway?" Jane asked.

"Jake," he said.

"Jane?" she asked.

"Jake. With a 'k.'"

"It would have been strange if you and I had both been called Jane," Jane noted.

"But for that 'k,' you might actually be me," Jake said.

Jane paused, raised an eyebrow, and then laughed. Jane's laugh was a revelation to Jake, and he barely felt worthy of it. He vowed to invent a series of better jokes that would actually deserve that laugh.

"Thank you, but it wasn't a very good joke," Jake said. "I'm not even sure it made much sense."

"Ah, but that's where the humor lay." Jane smiled sweetly.

Jake thought Jane was the coolest girl he had ever met.

Even though he had an exam the next morning, he took the long way back to the lab, a way that sent him past a certain hardware store. He pretended to be surprised to find himself in front of that hardware store. He pretended to be even more surprised when he went inside and bought thirty-six small lightbulbs.

And the next afternoon, when Jake Glass showed up at Jane's dorm with a brown paper bag filled with thirty-six antique lightbulbs, she pretended to be surprised to see him, too.

"I wanted to see how it would look all lit up." Jake smiled shyly and looked at his hands.

"You're a completist," Jane said.

"Something like that."

They went inside and screwed in the lightbulbs and plugged the sign into the wall. Jake switched the sign on, and the two sat on Jane's extra-long twin and stared at the restored MARGARETTOWN CINE-MAS sign.

"It's certainly bright," Jane said.

"Who's Margarettown?" Jake asked after a while.

Jane looked at him quizzically. "It's strange that you should say 'who.'"

"Why?"

"Most people would ask 'where,' but it is a 'who' actually. My mother was called Margaret Towne. She owned a store that sold broken things that other people sometimes tried to put back together."

That night, alone in her extra-long twin, Jane thought of Jake. In life, Jane reflected, the most interesting things tend to happen when you are on your way to do something else.

II.

When Jane was twenty-two, she decided to cut her hair. The week before she cut her hair, she had asked Aunt Bess the following question: "Am I like my mother?"

By way of response, Aunt Bess had said that Jane's mother had had long hair like Jane, but that her mother's hair had been red. (Like Gato, Jane thought to herself.) Aunt Bess had gone on to say that Jane's father had been particularly fond of the color. She also mentioned that Jane's mother had dyed her hair and that, on some level, Jane's father had felt betrayed when he found out. Aunt Bess had wondered how much of Jane's father's initial attraction to Jane's mother had been based on his belief that Jane's mother was a redhead.

It was then that Jane came up with the idea to cut off all her hair as a test for Jake. If he seemed very upset that her hair had changed, he didn't love her. If he didn't notice that her hair had changed, he didn't love her. If he accepted her new hair in a supportive and reasonable manner, he loved her. It was a simple test of love.

When Jake saw Jane's new hair, he kissed her all over her shorn head, and then they had sex. Jane deemed his reaction both supportive and reasonable.

While they were lying in bed that night, Jane made a decision: she would choose Jake above all others, even the ones she hadn't met yet. She suspected that he was the best one.

12.

When Jane was twenty-five, she married Jake.

There were three weddings scheduled in the church that day. Jane and Jake's was the second. Consequently, their ceremony could begin no earlier than 2:00 P.M., and they had to be completely out (including posed pictures!) by 3:30 P.M. It occurred to Jane that the tightness of the schedule didn't allow much room for dramatic pauses or doubt.

As Jane's primary caregiver, Aunt Bess was supposed to walk Jane down the aisle. Unfortunately, Aunt Bess had broken her leg in the final round of a limbo contest on a gay cruise that past spring. At first, Jane decided that no one would walk her down the aisle in Aunt Bess's place. However, it became clear that Aunt Libby, though not Jane's aunt in the biological sense, would like very much to be asked to stand in. When Jane finally did ask, Aunt Libby cried and said how much she loved Jane. Jane was pleased to have made Aunt Libby so happy, but in private she said to Jake, "One gay aunt or the other. I doubt anyone else will notice the difference anyway." It was true actually; Aunt Libby and Aunt Bess looked almost exactly alike; one was a bit rounder and the other was a bit longer, and only very close friends and family bothered to make the distinction.

A small room in the back of the church was reserved for brides to ready themselves. When Jane went to claim this room, she found the bride from the previous wedding still in there.

"Oh excuse me," the other bride said. "I guess I should be out of here by now."

Jane shrugged. "Take your time. I'm pretty much ready anyway." As Jane watched the other bride pack her things, it occurred to Jane that the other bride's wedding dress looked almost exactly like Jane's. Both dresses were off-white, strapless, A-line, and satin, with a train. The more Jane looked at the dress, the more it looked exactly like her own.

"It doesn't really matter, but I think we're wearing the same dress," Jane said.

The other bride looked at Jane's dress. "Hey, I think we might be!" She and Jane stared at each other's dresses. "The thing is, though, it's hard to tell. The more I look at your dress, the more I forget what mine even looked like to begin with," said the other bride.

To get a better perspective, the two brides crowded side by side in front of the full-length mirror that was propped in one corner of the room. After scrutinizing the two other brides in the mirror, both brides concluded that they were indeed wearing the same dress.

"It's strange," Jane said, looking at the two reflected brides. "Now there're four of us in this room wearing this dress."

The other bride laughed. Jane noticed that the other bride looked a lot like her, too. The other bride had dirty-blond hair like Jane and a heart-shaped face like Jane and amber eyes like Jane, too.

"I bet I could send you down the aisle instead of me, and no one would even know the difference," Jane said. "You could be my decoy, my counterfeit bride."

The other bride laughed again. "All brides look a bit the same, don't they, Jane? When it comes down to it, we're all just silly, young girls in silly, white dresses."

Outside the chapel in the narthex, a radiant Aunt
Libby clutched Jane's arm. "This is so exciting, darling!" Aunt Libby said. "I was engaged twice, but I
was never married, you know, and now it almost
feels like I'm getting married myself!"

Jane stared at the wooden floors of the church,
waiting for her cue. The floors were scuffed and
scratched. Well worn, Jane couldn't help thinking,
by all the brave and foolish souls who had engaged
in similar leaps of faith.

Softly, Aunt Libby whispered in Jane's ear, "It is
soon! It is soon! It is soon!" Her voice echoed
through the church, "Soon soon soon soon soon."
From the organ, a familiar refrain began to play.

As she walked down the aisle, Jane found herself thinking, not of Jake, but of her own parents.
She remembered a certain time, long ago when she
was young. Her parents had been throwing a party
(it may have been a birthday party for a relative of
her father's—a cousin? an uncle, perhaps?), and
Jane was meant to be in bed hours before. From her
perch at the top of the stairs, she had watched the

event—her mother, charming in a low-necked white blouse and pearls; her father, boyish in a slightly rumpled tuxedo. They had seemed familiar, but foreign, like actors hired to portray her parents. At the end of the night, when all the guests had left, her mother had removed all of her clothes except for a single high-heeled pump, and her parents had made love in the living room. Jane had found the lovemaking to be the most boring part of the evening by far and she had quickly fallen asleep. In her early years (before orthodontia), she was an extremely loud snorer. As soon as the sex was finished, her snores had alerted her parents that Jane was not in bed.

Jane had woken to the sound of her parents' voices. She had looked through the slats of the banister, but she could no longer see either adult.

"Do you think she saw the whole thing?" Jane had heard her mother ask.

"Even if she did, I doubt she understood it anyway," her father had answered.

And then Jane could hear footsteps on the stairwell—someone was coming up. And a second later, a human shadow on the wall—whether the shadow was her father or her mother, it was too soon to say. In point of fact, she would never know. For at that moment, Jane had decided to make a run for it back to her bedroom.

Coincidentally, Jane was considering a similar course of action as she made her way down the aisle. Yet, as long as the wedding march kept playing, Jane felt compelled to place one foot in front of the other. It occurred to Jane that there was a reason the wedding song was a *march* and not, say, a *waltz*.

By the time she arrived at the altar, Jane felt as if everyone else in the church had disappeared, as if she and Jake were the only people in the entire world, as if Jake might even be able to hear her thoughts.

Jane thought, You don't know me. And if you did, that might very well be the end of love.

And after a moment, Jake responded, Maybe, maybe not.

It isn't too late to—

Look, Jane, he interrupted, love is usually finite, but still worthwhile for as long as it lasts.

Is that meant to be comforting?

Yes, it is.

Jane thought, One day I might even hate you.

And Jake responded, But this is not that day. At least I hope it isn't.

So Jane laughed. When it came time to speak, she knew what she would say.

ACKNOWLEDGMENTS

Thanks to the amazing staff of Miramax Books: Kristin Powers, JillEllyn Riley, Claire McKinney, Kathy Schneider, Andrew Bevan and Caroline Clayton, who have all taken such wonderful care of my book. Thanks to John del Gaudio, Kate Terry, Janine O'Malley and Courtney Barr (nee Engelbrecht) for anecdotes, friendship and fonts. Thanks to Shana Kelly, Tracy Fisher, Eugenie Furniss, Anna DeRoy, Stuart Gelwarg, Elizabeth Urso, Elisabeth Ruge and Carolyn Caughey for more things than I can name. Above all, I am grateful to my editor, Jonathan Burnham, who is game for anything; my agents, Jonathan Pecarsky and Andy McNicol, who make it all happen; and my partner, Hans Canosa, who has been pushing those twins together for years.